Metaphorosis

December 2021

Beautifully made speculative fiction

Also from Metaphorosis

Metaphorosis

December 2021

edited by
B. Morris Allen

ISSN: 2573-136X (online)
ISBN: 978-1-64076-213-8 (e-book)
ISBN: 978-1-64076-214-5 (paperback)

Metaphorosis
a magazine of speculative fiction
from
Metaphorosis Publishing

Neskowin

December 2021

Orla, Always

Thomas Ha

She raised her head to listen for the rustle of his whispers.

It was always the same muttered words that she could never fully comprehend, followed by the sound of his hands—those callused, filth-crusted fingers tapping across the surface of the cellar door, feeling the wood for the lock and handle.

Even in the pitch of the underground, she could smell the crisp morning and knew to shut her eyes as searing white light spilled in around him, waiting for the creak of the door to seal in the darkness again, then for the pounding of his footfalls down the stone steps. She sensed the moment when he settled in the chair across from her bed, the clatter of his lantern on the ground telling her it was safe to look at him if she wanted.

But Orla could never raise her eyes to his.

Something about the sagging skin and darkened lines of his face bittered the back of her tongue with bile. Every time he visited, it seemed to Orla that he'd aged more than she remembered—shocks of gray sprouting at his temples and speckling the stubble of his beard, and the dewiness of his disheveled brow that told her that the simplest tasks were beginning to tire him more than before. It meant that the day she would be free of him was fast approaching, and if she were quiet and careful enough, she just might find the right moment to take that freedom.

Until then, she waited calmly, taking the bowl of stew he had brought her and drinking from one of its unchipped edges.

"I've been thinking," Orla said, pacing herself between mouthfuls. "About the last time we went for a walk, out there."

She watched him shift like he was struggling to hear her, or maybe to see her clearly in the mix of shadow and light, and because it disturbed her to look at his face, Orla in turn focused, as she often did, on his throat, just to the side of the point of swallowing, where the hint of a pulse quivered in the lantern's glow.

"I thought it'd be nice, one of these days, if we could walk again." She put the bowl on the floor when she was finished. "Maybe through the village, away from the Erst Field, even? Wherever the king's watchmen will allow us to go. It's just... been so long since I've seen the outside."

He said nothing, but she knew his mind was beginning to turn, that he had a fondness for their walks and craved the idea of a time when he didn't keep her locked away.

"You could tie my hands with rope," she went on. "And bind yourself to me with the other end. I won't run this time. I promise." She pushed her mouth to smile and forced her voice higher, to set him at ease.

And while he seemed to consider the notion, lost somewhere in his thoughts, or perhaps remembering something else from before, Orla felt under the wool and straw beneath her for the shard that she kept, the one she had wrenched free from the wooden bed frame during the quiet hours of the day when he disappeared.

It had taken countless cuts and splinters across the soft pads of her hands to pry apart the cracks in the grain in just the right way, until she had a fragment that she could wield. But now it was as if she could almost feel the light air outside enveloping her face, chilly and waiting, just for her. She squeezed the wood fragment in her throbbing, blistered hand and thought of the vast openness above her again and nothing between her and home.

The great, dark rock that would take her home.

"So?" she asked hopefully. "Can we walk together again?"

He did not move, or even blink, and he barely whispered the word.

"No."

Orla jumped from the bed and plunged the shard into his throat, and she allowed herself to look at him then, to take in the bare anguish that twisted across his face.

And she grinned, even as he roared and threw her against the stone wall.

She grinned, until she realized that she had missed.

That, aged and tired and hulking though he was, he had moved, just barely, catching the wood in the sinewy muscle just above his collar bone, where it protruded now as the blood spread under his shirt, hovering near the pulse in his throat, but not close enough.

The rage that flashed in his eyes, in that instant, frightened her deeply. It was an old anger she had rarely seen, that was reserved for the worst of things, but never, before, for her.

It was there now.

It might have been only a glimmer, but she knew that he would grab her by the neck and bash her against the stones.

So Orla crawled. She clambered backward, bending her limbs in the new ways as she moved to the ceiling, retreating to the corner, aloft where he could not pull her down. And though she was terrified, she dared not show it, instead widening the opening of her jaw.

She felt her second tongue squeeze its way through the canal of her throat and unfurl onto the wall, slapping wetly across the stones beneath her and dangling between them. She arched its end so that he could clearly see the curve of its barbs and would hesitate to reach for her, unless he wanted to feel her slice deep, flowing gashes across his arms.

No, he wouldn't dare try to hurt her now when she was like this.

He could only stand below, staring, so small in the lantern light, holding his wound and grunting in pain through his clenched teeth.

"Let me go *home*," she cried.

He looked at her strangely, pathetically, before turning to take the bowl, his heavy footfalls thumping again up each of the steps. He paused one last time to peer at her from the glow of his lantern across the dark space between them.

Then she shut her eyes as white flooded in from the open cellar door.

Brian sat for a time in the house, touching the wooden fragment embedded near his neck. He pulled steadily, sliding the shard out of his muscle bit by bit, blood dripping onto his shoulder and chest before he applied pressure with a cloth.

He tried to think of nothing else as he cleaned the wound, but he kept imagining

Orla, and her disquieting excitement as she leapt, that glee as she sank the shard into him, and the moment after, however brief, when he almost lashed out in return.

He wondered if Orla's mother could have kept the girl calm, but that only let in more unbidden thoughts. Brian rose to leave, even as his wound continued to bleed through the dressing.

He could only stay so long in those empty rooms.

The gray morning outside provided just enough sharpness to revive him, his breath misting as he stared at the cobblestones of the main road of Codladh village, until his eyes eventually met the figure of a man hunched in the doorway of another home.

The man looked back at Brian, his hands caked black with soil from working through the night. Brian could tell that he'd also just emerged from his cellar, and like all of the parents in Codladh, had come up just a bit darker in his face. Brian thought to say something, perhaps ask about the dig or how the other parents were doing, but the man's front door had already slid shut, just as the noise began.

It carried across the village, like the heavy echoing of giant bells that Brian had once heard in the cities—at least, that's how the noise always sounded to him. Others heard horses screaming, as if they'd been lashed, or the feverish rise of locusts chittering in the summer. But for Brian, it was only the bells, and when they came, he whispered the words he always said under his breath as they clanged, words repeated again and again to carry his mind through the moment, until the silence finally settled in around his ears again.

The morning chill remained for a while longer, and Brian squinted at the flashes of sun peeking through the dark sheets of clouds, until, eventually, a horse clopped near, its ears twitching from the flies gathering around its glossy, black body.

The king's soldier on its back leaned forward in his saddle and stared at Brian carefully, his clear eyes peering out above the cloth that covered his nose and mouth.

"Bit of trouble?" He spoke with a youthful, quavering voice and pointed to a few dots of blood that had seeped through Brian's bandage.

"No trouble."

The soldier cleared his throat.

"On with you, then."

Brian and his escort took the quickest path to the Erst Field, around the village's edge and along the curve of the main road. He ignored the soldiers lined around Codladh Square and positioned between the houses, their stares following him and all the other villagers who were going about their day with their heads bowed. The king's men had come to treat this like an ordinary plague town, wary of desperate runners who might break their barricade, but the truth was that no man or woman in Codladh was going to run.

Brian made it a point to nod to his neighbors as he passed, and he could tell each one was searching his face for signs of what might come of the dig. They looked to him for answers, now, because of what little they knew of his life before he came to the village.

When he first arrived those years ago, as an outsider, before Orla's mother took him in, when he still carried his experiences like poison, the people of Codladh had been distant with him, as they should have been.

But as time passed, and he learned to let his anger go, when Orla was born, he assumed, though he couldn't identify a particular moment, the others seemed to think of him more as one of their own. And he almost forgot that they had ever seen him as anything else.

Now, though, they needed that other part of him. They needed the outsider to tell them if this might be the day they finally buried the stone.

Everyone in Codladh knew they were almost to the end, now that the pit they had constructed had become quarry-like, deep and wide and buttressed by all manner of wooden framing, to the point where it was almost impossible to see all the way down to the bottom.

But Brian kept his expression impassive as ever, understanding that they all needed to guard themselves from hoping for too much or too little, that losing that balance would hurt the village worse than any affliction.

He continued beyond the edge of Codladh, where he would, on most days, walk the quarter mile to the flats and take up his post at the dig. But today he heard something he recognized coming just beyond the tall grass, almost muffled by the heaviness in the air, and he found himself heading toward it, neither hurrying nor slowing his pace.

"You! Where are you—Wait!"

His young escort called from his horse with increasing urgency as Brian kept walking further from the road. And when it was clear that Brian wasn't turning around, the escort followed, over a slope and down to a patchwork of dewy grass and muck, where they found a circle of men gathered, each of them in the dull leather uniform of the king's army, laughing as they stood around a covered tumbrel.

The group of soldiers jeered and chattered to one another until they gradually turned to see Brian come upon them. There was a flicker of uncertainty across the group—some of their hands floating down to their hilts and changing their stances—but that dissipated when they realized he was only a villager, and a few of their expressions, what he could see above the cloth strips covering their mouths, took a different cast.

Brian ignored them, looking beyond their figures and between the bars of the tumbrel and barely making out the slinking shape of an afflicted boy held captive in the cart.

The boy was no more than fourteen, pressing his shivering body against one of the corners of the cart, his arms wrapped around the wooden slats. The flaking cracks forming around the folds of his mouth hinted at muscles beginning to change their shape, and the whorls of skin that covered what were once his eyes left only shrunken pinholes to take in and shut out the light.

The afflicted boy sank further from the reach of the men, and through his torn clothing Brian could see the exposed lumps of bone growing on either side of the boy's ribs, the beginnings of the smaller arms that some of the other Codladh children grew in their final stages.

"*Home,*" the boy rasped, mucus dripping from the corner of his lips.

It was only a second, but Brian thought back to Orla—how there were moments, more and more frequent, when the cadence and lilt of her voice became unrecognizable that way—moments when she believed she was speaking but only made that same rasping, barking noise.

Brian studied the boy's face, noticing the small cuts where the child had been prodded.

"Move on," one of the men nearest to the tumbrel said. He seemed older than the others and had the serious affect of someone with authority.

"Home."

Brian looked to the older soldier and spoke so that everyone could hear him. "This boy...His name is Liam," he said. "Liam Conroy." He stepped forward, and because he was taller than most men, he cast a shadow that tended to make others attentive.

"His family lives on the far side of the square by the fallen wych elm," Brian continued. "His father is the apothecary, and his mother, Rosemary, tends to swine. They're good people, who care very much for their son."

Some of the soldiers shifted uneasily.

"Home."

"You don't...have to do anything more than this," Brian went on. "He's just a child."

The older soldier stared and touched the cloth over his mouth. "You keep on with your work, and we will with ours." He looked at the escort on horseback, as if to indicate that he'd best see Brian on his way, but the younger soldier seemed unsure what to do.

Brian closed his hand, and something small in him stirred, thinking of what could happen if he pressed the men.

He knew the soldiers looked at the parents, including Brian, with a queasy disdain. It didn't matter that Codladh was made of hardworking men and women, apothecaries and swineherds who loved their children dearly. That love alone lacked any real power, any strength, which was the only attribute of meaning to a soldier.

All they saw in the villagers were hollowed, pitiful creatures barely capable of digging in the fields, and the king's men despised them all the more for it.

Even so, Brian still knew the innerworkings of soldiers' minds, especially restless, overeager ones like these, and he felt there were other ways that this could go if he approached them with something of consequence, something that they comprehended.

"If this is the way it's to be, I understand," he said evenly, slowly, so that they had to lean into the words to follow him. "But...who do I say is responsible when the Thinling asks? I assume you." Brian gestured at the markings on the older man's pauldron, half-obscured by his wool cloak, and the soldier blinked rapidly.

"The Thinling?" He touched his shoulder, and the tenor of his voice changed.

"Yes. He's observing the dig, and we're meant to speak shortly."

The older man briefly turned to the escort on horseback, who gave the slightest nod, then he swallowed and scratched his ear before finally responding. "If that's true...that the Thinling's here...You can already see, this one is..."

"Still meant for the Thinling to study," Brian finished, without raising his voice. "And he doesn't like losing subjects for study. I can tell you that."

The murmuring among the men seemed to die in their throats. Some things had changed in the infantry over the years, but the palpable chill among the footmen at the mention of the Thinling was the same as it ever had been.

The older soldier looked at no one in particular, and Brian could see his halted breathing from the movement of the cloth on his face. "If that's how...if that's how the Thinling says he wants things, we'll follow that, of course." He waved to the men behind him, and a few lifted the rails of the tumbrel up from the mud.

"Of course," Brian repeated.

"By the wych elm, you said?"

Brian nodded.

The men began dragging the tumbrel toward Codladh, the large wheels wobbling through the inches of mud. The older soldier stopped at the slope, giving Brian a look before taking his leave, less of anger and more searching, like he was trying to understand why Brian's bearing wasn't quite like the others in Codladh.

But Brian's gaze stayed only on the boy who clutched the bars and looked back at him ponderously with the dark holes of what had once been his eyes, until the cart and the men eventually disappeared over the hill.

"And he arrives."

The Thinling called out as Brian and his escort approached the canvas tent. The king's physician rose from a planning table set outside, his unusually skinny frame stretching impossibly upward as he stood, tall in a way that always reminded Brian of a reflection distorted in cracked glass. On the table in front of him, the bloody remains of an animal streamed over the edges, seeping plops of wet mass onto the dirt, and the Thinling held up his hands, long, slender fingers doused in a fierce red that dripped to his elbows as he smiled.

The escort hesitated, his black horse slowing to a halting clop as they reached the end of the road, shaking its head anxiously at the smell of the blood.

Brian looked up at the young man reassuringly. "You've done your part now and don't need to be here for this."

The soldier's eyes darted away from the figure of the Thinling, and when he lowered the cloth over his mouth, revealing his smooth, beardless face, Brian realized the escort couldn't have been much older than Orla.

"Are you sure...you want to be alone?" the boy asked, a genuine concern tinging his voice under the trembling, reminding Brian vaguely of other men he knew who followed the king's flag.

"I'll be fine, son. Thank you. Go back to the others."

Brian reached up his hand, and the soldier clasped it. "May He bless the roads before you," the young man intoned.

"And may all the dark things die," Brian finished.

He watched the soldier trot his horse hurriedly to the path and away, then he turned back to the tent where the Thinling waited.

Simon Wayn, the name by which Brian had known the Thinling when they'd first met during the campaigns, grinned with large, unnaturally white teeth. The footmen back then had whispered that he was born of something unholy, and Brian wondered if there was some truth in the rumor, because Simon's face was just as it had been decades ago, like porcelain untouched by time.

They had first met outside a field tent not unlike this one, when Brian was barely old enough to hold a blade, still dark-haired and lean and without the weight in his heart he'd later carry, and he'd looked at the Thinling directly and without hesitation, even then, providing the latest reports on field movements that the physician had requested.

"Do you not fear me, soldier?" the pale man had asked him all those years ago, his unsettling eyes studying Brian's expression carefully.

"*No,*" Brian said simply, maybe foolishly in retrospect.

"*But surely you must find me strange? Something other than normal to someone like you, at least?*" he pressed, almost as though interrogating him.

"*There is, I think, nothing strange, or even normal for that matter, sir,*" Brian swallowed. "*Only what we know, and take for granted, and that we have yet to know, and fear.*"

And something about the answer seemed to please Simon in just the right way, because he gave the first of many smiles to Brian, chilling and practiced, that Brian would learn signaled a request to follow.

"*Tell me, young man. What do you know of the creatures that come from the otherworld?*"

The memory, and those words in particular, lingered with Brian in the present as the Thinling extended a blood-covered hand, unaware that there was anything curious in the gesture. Brian shook it, looking down at the limbless, open carcass on the table between them, its skin flayed completely from the weeping, pink muscle, and its lungs and heart churning slowly, the only sign it was somehow still barely alive.

The Thinling plucked a small sac from the body and held it up for a moment, then sucked it delicately into his mouth. He invited Brian to take a piece of his choosing, but Brian held up a hand to decline.

"The dig site," Brian said, looking away and waiting until the Thinling was done chewing. "Everything to your expectations, I hope?"

Simon licked his fingertips before dabbing his mouth with a handkerchief. "Very much so, I'd say," he returned to the bloody remains and tossed aside what seemed to be the wound cord of intestines onto the ground. "The pit will be deep enough soon, possibly today."

"And then we can begin?"

Simon looked up.

"Oh yes. And then we can begin."

Brian stared at the blighted expanse of the Erst Field in front of them, his eyes drawn across the flat plateau to the tall, jagged figure of the Slaking Stone, which was what the Thinling had come to call the dark rock over the course of his study. It stood ominously alone in the middle of the land and was, by Brian's estimation, at least the size of a fortified castle turret, stretching fifty feet or more into the air and growing ever so slightly with each day that passed.

Brian didn't need to look on it long, because he had seen every detail of its angular, obsidian body in his mind every day since it came to their village.

That creeping dawn when it first appeared—when men harrowing the soil stumbled upon it and called all of Codladh to see—the faithful had claimed it was a Godsent artifact, or some kind of blessing crystal from the old folktales, bestowing good fortune to the village.

But Brian, who stood far back from others in the crowd at the Erst Field that day, had already known.

He'd seen enough in his younger days to recognize an otherworldly creature like this one.

And so Brian sent his first letters to the king's court immediately, doing his best to describe the dark rock: its measurements, its properties, his assumption that its elemental fundament was perhaps of the earth, given its appearance. It had been some time since he had contacted the capital, years since he left to begin his quieter life in Codladh, but he hadn't known where else to turn with something of this nature. *Send men*, he had written, *because it won't be long before it begins to prey on the minds of the people living here*. But, even then, he couldn't have anticipated how quickly the sickness would fall on Codladh after that.

It had started with a noise.

A booming, like the clang of a bell deeper than any he'd heard before, a noise so penetrating it entered his mind and covering his ears did nothing to dampen it. It was so painful that it woke him suddenly in the night and caused him to stumble through the dark, searching for Orla, but finding her nowhere in their home. His shouts were soon joined by others outside as he wandered into the road. Fathers, mothers, were screaming their children's names, unable to find them in their beds or around their houses. He went with the throng of others, floating lanterns glowing in the night as they all moved outward from the village, until, of course, among the waves of wheat that still grew in the Erst Field at the time, they saw the boys and girls of Codladh gathered in a ring around the Slaking Stone, hands outstretched.

Brian still remembered Orla standing in her night shirt, her eyes half closed, sleepily smiling at her father.

"*What's wrong?*" Orla had whispered as Brian clutched her to his chest. "*What's wrong?*"

Brian closed his hand tightly as he stared at the stone and thought of her.

"How is the girl?" Simon asked, bringing Brian out of his memories as he looked back from the field. The Thinling inserted his fingers back into the body before him, exploring the cavernous spaces under the ribs.

"The same," Brian answered.

"Really?" Simon tilted his head one way and then the other, lifting another organ and prodding it with thin fingertips. "She should be well along, I would think. If you'd like me to take a look—"

"No!" Brian said, then softened his voice. "It's fine. We're fine."

Simon's eyes rested on the patches of blood near the collar of Brian's shirt, where his injury had seeped over the course of the morning.

Brian touched it and cleared his throat. "Fine, I said."

The Thinling's face was unreadable, but he returned to pulling apart the carcass, and Brian let out a small breath.

"My men have finished the sledge," Simon nodded to the other end of the Erst Field, and Brian could barely see the large platform of planks and wheels that had been constructed. "Once the Slaking Stone's dragged over to the pit, we can bury it, finally, just as we discussed."

The method for killing the creature had been worked out between them in the early months, before the king's army could redirect men from the Mist Bridges to the countryside for support. Brian had written more urgent letters when the affliction started showing itself in earnest, only in the children for some reason.

It was only ever in the children.

The boys and girls began forgetting things, becoming agitated at the mention of their names, lashing out when others got too close. And every time the noise from the stone rang through the village, whether day or night, the children turned their heads toward the Erst Field, like animals hearing a call.

Home.

Brian recalled Orla's face, twisted and distorted in a way he'd never seen it, raging as he shut the cellar doors on her, because there was no other way to keep her from being drawn to the rock in the middle of the night.

"*Let me go home! Let me go!*" she screamed. He had felt the pressure of her hands beating against the other side of the bouncing wood, stronger than ever before, and pushed back with all his might. Brian had wept that first time, bolting the cellar door shut, the sound of screeching metal joining the inhuman wailing coming from below.

The Thinling had his theories about what was happening to the children. *The form this otherworlder has taken—I don't believe it's even rock. What you describe seems more like the cocoon of a metamorph to my mind*, Simon wrote. His first letters to Brian were warm, eager to connect over the subject of otherworlders, almost blithely unaware of the pain Brian and his neighbors were suffering. *Something else, something worse, is being birthed from within the Slaking Stone.*

The Thinling believed young ones, being the most vulnerable and persuadable in thought, were the ideal candidate for the rock to subsume, and that their transformation aided its development. Maybe the vile barbs and limbs, the violent tendencies, the inexorable draw of the children to the Erst Field, were meant to serve the stone in its defense while it gestated. Or maybe the physical alterations were echoes of the form the otherworlder itself was going to take next, and the changes were a side effect of its deep hold on the children's minds.

Simon's correspondence appended ink illustrations of what the dark rock might contain, nightmarish studies of many-limbed creatures with dripping carapaces and segmented bodies, things that Brian could hardly believe the Thinling could stand to envision, let alone reproduce.

But regardless of the cause or meaning of the transformations in the children, the men and women of Codladh did everything they could think of to treat or reverse them. Tonics, leeches, sweat baths, but nothing productive came of it, and the children grew steadily worse. Several parents tried leaving Codladh with their young ones in tow, hoping that distance from the dark rock would bring them to their senses. But they all found they couldn't go more than a mile before the children started screaming and writhing in pain, as if their innards were being raked by glass.

Others turned to destroying the stone itself, as if they had the means for such a thing—setting fire to the field or slinging pickaxes and blades to crack it apart. But the dark exterior of the otherworlder remained completely unmarred, no matter what was done.

That's because its affinity isn't of the earth, Simon had written after a number of further exchanges. *The way its sound flows, its control over the children within a distance. It's of the air, I'd wager. That's how the transformative affliction works through them.* Brian could see the Thinling's excitement in the flourishes of the ink. *So to kill it, we will have to take that air away.*

Simon's letter enclosed a diagram, a side view of a pit roughly a hundred feet deep. He drew ladders, support platforms, and timber to keep the walls of the pit stable. And above the hole, Simon had designed a set of beams and pulleys, spidering down with ropes and buckets, so that men at the mouth of the pit could set aside the soil sent up to them by the diggers.

As always, Simon thought of every last detail.

And, as he had in years past, Brian took the Thinling's plans and organized the work to make them real, acting as the hand to Simon's thoughts, building and executing the contraptions that the Thinling designed in his madness.

In doing so, Brian recalled, familiarly more than fondly, the time he had previously spent as one of the king's Cullers after that fateful first meeting with Simon outside of that tent—a service as one of the men selected by the Thinling to identify, study, entrap, and destroy otherworldly things that invaded from beyond the Mist Bridges.

It was a part of himself he had all but smothered, and he felt a kind of misery and, if he were being honest with himself, perhaps a small fervor, in having to surface it again. But no matter what he was feeling or not feeling about the past, Brian, like the rest of Codladh, would do whatever was necessary to see this through.

The fathers and mothers whose families were affected by the affliction volunteered for the dig site first, taking up the shovels and buckets to carve out the ditch just beyond the field. The rest of the untouched, either too young or too old for children of their own, began providing supplies for the village's project.

And now, after weeks and months of toiling, here they stood, finally on the cusp of destroying the Stone.

The Thinling drew back his lips, flashing his red-stained teeth with the eagerness he always showed when they reached this moment before they hunted an otherworlder down.

"There is just...one more thing, Brian," he said, pulling vigorously at the carcass. "The sledgemen haven't been able to approach the Slaking Stone as of late. It keeps filling the field with that...noise when anyone gets close. The pain it causes at that distance is unbearable, or so my men tell me." He laughed, and held up a round, black piece of tissue from the animal that Brian did not recognize. "But...I've been working on something to help with that."

The Thinling reached into the drawers of the planning table. He brought up a wineskin with one hand, removing the cap with his teeth and holding it under Brian's nose.

The odor made him draw back and gasp from the sharpness of it.

"Dwale?" Brian coughed, vaguely remembering the burning stench from the battlefield, when the physicians would drench wounds and make men drink it before they went under the knife.

The Thinling nodded. "Barrow swine gall, henbane, opium and a few other touches." He picked up the round black flesh and squeezed it over the opening of the wineskin, letting a stream of dark juice spill into the pouch before capping it again. "If we can apply enough of this to the creature's body—fill some of the cracks and narrows of it with the dwale— it will sleep so deeply that its noises will subside for several days, at least. That will give us the time we need to drag it to the pit and put it to rest, once and for all. If... someone can get to it, that is."

Simon looked pointedly at Brian, and he understood what he was asking of him, having been tasked like this many times before. Brian had always been Simon's favorite to use for kills like these, because the Thinling believed that the otherworlders came from an unstable plane of the intangible. And while they took a strange pleasure in forming in this physical world, twisting and reshaping things for their own amusement, they were ultimately, at their core, creatures of the mind. So it took people of equanimity, of unshakable thought and heart like Brian, to defeat them. Or those were just the lies the Thinling told to lure others into his work; Brian supposed that he would never really know.

And truthfully, it mattered little to Brian in the moment, as he took the wineskin from the Thinling's long fingers and squeezed the pouch.

"We all still wonder, at court, you know," Simon brushed his pale hair from his eyes with bloody fingers. "Whether you might return to this someday. After all, there's not much in a place like this for men like us, is there?"

Brian hesitated, thinking of what he might say to the Thinling in response. He wondered, momentarily, if he could perhaps make the Thinling understand why he had left the Cullers all those years ago, how he had found more meaning in this place than in any of the hunts or battles or marches under the king's flag.

But he knew Simon was too set in his views, about men he used for fodder and about villages like these, and Brian realized it wouldn't make any difference in the end.

So he remained silent, nodding in thanks for the dwale before moving beyond the table.

"And may all the dark things die," Simon smiled.

"And may all the dark things die," Brian answered, heading toward the destitute flatland, where the Slaking Stone waited.

The moment Brian stepped onto the field, he felt the deep, clanging noise begin. The sound overtook him and flooded deep into his stomach, almost as if the stone understood what was coming and was trying, instinctively, to push it away.

The ringing in Brian's ears gradually began to shift in sensation to something he had never experienced, like the touches of insects crawling somewhere behind his eyes and down into the soft point at the back of his throat, choking him from within.

He ignored the feeling—believing it was the stone trying to disturb and unsettle him—and resisted his body's instincts to gag or tear at himself. Instead, he continued, step by step, across the field.

The closer he came, the larger the otherworlder loomed, and he could see more clearly, along the base of the rock, the stone-fused bodies of the children who had escaped their cellars to what they had told their tearful parents was "*Home*," this skeletal embrace that absorbed their changed blood and flesh, until only pieces of them lining the rock remained. Simon believed that by drinking them, the creature was softening its shell, preparing to emerge in its next form when enough of their bodies had merged.

Brian tried not to look at the faces pressed to the black surface as he walked ahead.

Another booming sound filled his head then, and he fell, drops of blood raining from his nose onto the deadened soil. The world swayed, like everything was pulling away under him, and he had to shut his eyes before he could rise to his feet.

The stone was in his thoughts now, he knew, as he reached the midpoint of the Erst Field, because it began to invade his vision with impossible figures, the way otherworlders sometimes liked to do. He could see shadows of men walking in the field that he gradually realized were echoes of dead and dying things he had seen long ago when he fought for the king, in distant lands near the base of the Mist Bridges, where the otherworlders stalked freely, like merciless lords, bending the people they encountered to their will to become mindless servants who would slaughter others in their name. Dripping limbs, arrow-filled faces, men with severed fingers, scraping at his boots.

But Brian walked ahead, forcing the shapes to fade to blurs in the corners of his vision as he advanced toward the stone, relegating those violent shades to his memories again.

The booming grew to an aching roar as he got even closer, just within reach, and an immense pressure squeezed somewhere inside of him. He felt he was sinking into the freezing blackness of the sea, weighted chains around his neck, and he collapsed wholly, unable to bring himself to rise.

A burning spread through Brian's lungs as the world began to whirl, and he almost felt he might succumb to panic. But he reminded himself that, like all else, these feelings were illusory, and he turned his mind to his breathing, concentrating on its rhythm, until he found his center of balance again.

The spinning subsided, and he found purchase with his fingers, lifting himself just enough to dig his elbows into the soil and steady his knees.

Then, finally, he stood at the Slaking Stone, observing the blur of his own body reflected in its glassy surface, and the relentless hollow noise softened to a dull and distant hum. The creature couldn't speak, as far as they knew, but at this close distance, Brian could sense, as much as he could in any other injured, living thing, that, more than anything else in that moment, it was afraid.

There were sudden flickers of images bursting in Brian's thoughts that he believed to be the stone seeping further into his head—images of the king's soldiers, dragging the Slaking Stone to the sledge, and casting its body deep, down, decisively, into the pit Codladh had made. Cascading sheets of earth pounded on top of it in the hole, over and over, until all light was blocked out from above, and the stone felt nothing but a black, crushing weight.

And then it showed him the children, showed him Orla, screaming in the cellars across the village, crying out like they were being pressed down and strangled by something unseen.

Brian held his breath.

He saw Orla huffing rapidly, her cheek against the stone floor, until her breathing slowed to a deflated stop, and her wet eyes looked on lifelessly ahead.

The message from the Slaking Stone was clear.

If you kill me, they will die.

Brian had known otherworlders to bargain like this, close to the end. They were never any different than men in that way, no matter how they tried to disguise it. But whether the stone was lying to save itself or telling the truth about what its death would do, it made no meaningful difference, Brian knew. All that mattered, all that ever mattered, was whether Brian did everything he could for Orla and the others, while there was still time.

Brian looked back at the jagged planes of dark rock, unblinking, and decided, if they were somehow connected in this way, that he would try to show it something else.

He concentrated on the image of Orla, as she was before she became sick, when she smiled sweetly and rested her cheek on his chest when she embraced him. He recalled her stumbling as a young girl on the shores of the Codladh river, giggling as she slipped on the smooth stones and regained her balance, cold water dripping from her chin as she laughed.

And he imagined Orla's mother, years before she passed. He remembered when she had taken him in, when he was weary and first found his way to the village, and she cared for him until he remembered how to care for himself. He remembered how he finally learned to sleep by her side through the night without waking. How she sat near the crackling fireplace, gently touching her swelling, pregnant belly. And how, later, she held their child in the crook of her arm—that pink face barely peeking out from the folds of blankets—and she whispered the words, those same words, that Brian still repeated to himself under his breath each day. *"My sweet girl."*

This, Brian thought, sending his intentions to the dark rock, not knowing whether it could feel any fraction of what Brian had felt, if it could even understand what he was showing it.

This is forever. No matter what may come. No matter what happens to her. No matter what happens to me.

This is forever. Do you understand?

And in the seconds after, there was nothing Brian felt from the rock in return —no image, or pain, or form of retort— just an overwhelming sense of bewilderment over the memories.

Because, of course, the creature would never comprehend any of what Brian felt, not really. Much like the Thinling, and the king's soldiers, and any of the others who might sneer at everything a village like Codladh was and had to offer, they would never, could never, understand the meaning and power in these ordinary things.

In that moment, Brian realized, above all, he pitied them for it.

He opened the wineskin and poured the dwale across the cracks of the Slaking Stone, watching the liquid spread and sink into the crevices. And he felt a shuddering, a dimming of the otherworlder deep within his mind as it sank into a darkness from which it would never emerge, before a silence, heavy and welcome, finally fell over the field.

Orla turned back and looked at the cellar door.

She heard nothing and was unsure what she had been listening for.

In fact, she was almost certain that the door she was seeing wasn't real and that she'd long since fallen asleep, because she could still sense her body, ungainly and leaden and almost unfamiliar, pressed against the bed, in the dark, as her mind continued to drift.

But the cellar door in her dream, the one in front of her now, opened as if it were always meant to lead her away, out into a gray afternoon where the sun's warmth seemed determined to stay out of reach. And somewhere, beyond the door and a village square and an unmarked field, Orla imagined a pit, strange and unnatural, stretching so far and so deep that it could swallow a mountain.

And she saw a man there, pacing toward the chasm—a man Orla knew well, somehow, she was all but sure. His heavily-lined face, creased brow, those downturned shoulders, it all meant something to her, even if she couldn't grasp it just then.

She watched as he passed a group of villagers working pulleys at the mouth of the pit, buckets rising and falling in rhythm, and he descended the ladder to the first platform, then another, to the next. And things grew dimmer around him as he went further below, until there was only a distant circle of stifled light above, cut by the wood support beams like a fractured window to a world that didn't seem to exist.

Near him, one of the other men, with eyes sleepless and dark, handed him a shovel, and he turned to take up a position between the rest of them.

She watched as he bent low and scraped and bent low and scraped—his muscle and bone seeming to spread something of a chill, but the heat from a fresh wound near his neck throbbing, keeping him moving and reaching.

Again and again.

Filling the bucket closest to him, he whispered softly in time with the scraping of the metal sliding into the dirt.

Again and again.

"My sweet girl," he said, almost in recitation, like he knew no one would hear him.

"My sweet girl."

Something about the words felt familiar —as if she'd heard them every day of her life, whispered in her ear, or at her bedside, or through the cellar door.

"My sweet girl," the man said, as he reached and pulled the dirt from the ground, his fingers mottled with blisters and blood and dirt.

Again and again.

"My sweet girl."

And above them in the distance, she saw a black, jagged rock, larger than any of the houses in the village, larger than anything Orla remembered seeing, dragged on a massive sledge over to the pit's open mouth by dozens of oxen and men. As it neared the site, the diggers emerged, slowly climbing the scaffolds and ladders to the edge. They joined together in the shouting and shoving, straining and screaming, some doing their best to hold back tears as it took everything in all of them to move the rock.

The villagers gave the wheeled sledge one final push, down and over into the hole, and there was a thunderous echo that seemed to shake the world as the dark thing plummeted into the emptiness below. It crashed through the wide beams and tangle of rope and pulleys, and soil ruptured and spilled from the unstable sides of the pit as the cavernous hole partially swallowed itself, the stone finally disappearing from sight in the waves of all that shadow and earth.

Orla watched the men and women standing there above the chasm, their faces breaking with a pained relief, and she drifted across those people, one by one, their names and other little recollections of them seeping slowly back to her. Until she found that man again, the one she'd recognized from before, now standing at the pit's edge with the rest.

Her thoughts stayed with him as he looked down into the darkness, at a deep nothing beneath him, his fingers still reaching below slightly, out of instinct and habit borne of hours and days and weeks of all that digging.

And somehow, Orla knew, even when she woke shortly after, confused and in pain, looking up at the cellar door, still closed.

She knew, even as she felt her senses return, and her body began to seem less strange and separate, joining again with her mind, as if they'd never been apart.

She knew that her father would be waiting somewhere, at the other side of the door.

And no matter what happened next, he would still be there, reaching out for her, always.

See Thomas Ha's story "Orla, Always" online at Metaphorosis.
If you liked it, leave a comment. Authors love that!
Remember to subscribe to our e-mail updates so you'll know when new stories are posted.

About the story

I mainly wanted to write about losing a loved one to an influence beyond your control, the pain and animosity that can accompany that kind of gradual loss, and your inability (especially if you're a parent estranged from a child) to let go of the hope that you'll reconnect, which can be risky, if not outright dangerous. I've written other stories with similar themes, and they do not always end well. This one arguably does, depending on your view of the ending.

I also wanted to create a stark fantasy world with a traditional good versus evil construct (i.e., the king's army and the otherworlders), but where both sides are brutal, and where it's really ordinary people, like Codladh's villagers, with their devotion and resilience, who make a difference. Instead of a bombastic battle to win the day, I wanted to write a less common kind of conflict where physical violence was not necessarily the key.

And lastly, I just really wanted something weird. Knights versus aliens was my original concept. Something humans might think of as demonic or hellish but is actually quite strange and difficult for people to understand and confront—a sentient rock or a mystical disease, instead of a horned monster. The otherworlders are never confirmed as aliens, but I imagine them as interdimensional creatures of some kind, with motives that are almost beyond comprehension. What I was interested in exploring was, how do good, ordinary people, with everything to lose, endure and survive in the face of something like that?

A question for the author

Q: How has your writing evolved over time?

A: I'm working on being more judicious with my writing. I have a tendency to over-explain my characters and their motivations, so I'm learning to trust my readers more by paring some of that back. Similarly, while my stories vary in genre and style, I'm beginning to home in on subjects that matter to me personally, so I think a kind of consistency is slowly forming in a small body of work. But, like many folks, I am still very much a work in progress, so I have a lot yet to figure out.

About the author

Thomas Ha is a former attorney turned stay-at-home father who enjoys writing speculative fiction during the rare moments when all of his kids are napping at the same time. Thomas grew up in Honolulu and, after a decade plus of living in the northeast, now resides in Los Angeles.

thomashawrites.com, @ThomasHaWrites

Dry Season

Caite Sajwaj

The Ozarks haven't seen rain in nearly five years. All the well-to-do folks from Springfield to Fayetteville moved away after the first year. Now, the tourists are gone, and the lake's dried up to nothing more than a craterous puddle. In the town of Sunrise Beach, Missouri, the children ride sleds down the parched shore. They dig in the sand for bones and beer tabs and lost jewelry.

It's June. Before the dry season, the town would've been packed to the gills with drunk tourists. They'd spill onto the streets from every restaurant and dive bar and pool hall, reeking of beer and Banana

Boat tanning oil. But, this year, there are no tourists.

At Redhead's Pizzeria, Janie Rivas, who isn't a redhead but a brunette, stands behind the cash register, vigorously chewing a stick of Big Red. Janie's lived in Sunrise Beach all her life. She doesn't particularly mind the lack of tourists, though she could use the tips. Two weeks ago, Janie got her acceptance letter from the University of Washington, and the cost of living in Seattle isn't anything to sneeze at. But her only customers today are the remaining three city counselors and they've never left more than 10%. So, instead of refilling their water glasses, Janie just listens to their conversation.

"What if it never rains again?" Myrna Fairway asks. Myrna owns Gator's Waterfront Grill. Her last customer was a young man passing through on his way to Denver, and he didn't even order anything, just asked to use her bathroom.

"It has to rain sometime," Lou Conaway says. He's 83, and he's spent his whole life in Sunrise Beach. To Lou, the last five years are nothing, a pothole on an otherwise smooth road.

"Well, *when* is sometime, Lou?" asks Mayor Cobb. "The town is dying. Hell, we don't even have a beach anymore! We have to do something *now*." Cobb works in the post office. His annual mayoral salary is $1, but there's something about that title—*mayor*. He's afraid he'll soon be mayor of nothing.

"What're we supposed to do?" Lou asks. "This is *the weather* we're talking about."

"You know very well what we're supposed to do," Myrna says quietly.

Lou curses.

"She's right," Mayor Cobb says. "We have to make an offering."

They take a vote, but it's just a formality. Myrna and Mayor Cobb have been on the city council together for three decades, and the only time they've broken ranks is when Myrna voted to rename Main Street "Sunrise Street," and Mayor Cobb voted to rename it after himself. But this isn't about vanity. This is about survival. And so, Janie listens to them decide, 2-1, that the town of Sunrise Beach will make an offering, whatever that is.

The next day, Mayor Cobb issues a proclamation and the townspeople gather at the docks. Janie isn't among them. She's tethered to one of the beams, watching dawn sunlight gleam off the ancient remains of broken beer bottles, still half-buried in the lakebed. Sun-bleached driftwood juts from the sand, like the bones of a monstrous sea creature or the pillars of a long-lost temple. Janie is still wearing her work-shirt from the pizzeria.

The townspeople watch and wait. Soon, the dry season will be over, and the air will hum with the sounds of motorboats and churning water. At one point, a man shouts, "I think I felt a drop!" But it's only sweat that dripped from his forehead. An hour later, there's still no rain. The sky is the clear, bright blue of a gas fire. Eventually, the crowd begins to thin. The citizens of Sunrise Beach have lives to get back to. They have morning shifts starting soon. They have children that need to be dropped off at daycare. And they expected something exciting to happen, something *spectacular*—a torrential downpour of Old Testament proportions, perhaps. But offerings are not miracles. Offerings take time, and the people of Sunrise Beach have grown bored. One by one, they file away, until only Janie is left.

She stares out across the lake bed. The dirt is dry and brittle and laced with shallow fissures, like a crust of brown bread split in the oven. Morning turns to midday and, still, the rain doesn't come. *This is all bullshit*, Janie thinks. Just superstition. Any minute now, the city council will realize they've made a huge mistake. "Sorry for the trouble," they'll say, and give Janie a nice chunk of change so she doesn't go running her mouth. She'll move to Washington like she planned. There are no droughts in Washington. Then, she feels it, cold and sharp as a bullet. *Rain.*

It comes slow at first, then fast. Water pools at the bottom of the lake, settling into the cracks and creases in the dirt. Janie starts to cry, but she doesn't call for help. The townspeople will be here soon enough, and it won't be to help her. No, they'll flock to the shore to chant and cheer and dance in the rain. Some of the children have never even *seen* rain before. Their parents will bring them outside to stomp in the puddles.

Janie writhes and shimmies, trying to slip from her bindings. When that doesn't work, she jerks and screams and kicks the ancient wooden beams of the dock. But this dock has stood over a hundred years, and it'll likely stand for a hundred more. Janie, by her best estimates, won't last more than a few hours. She wonders if she'll end up drowning to death or if whatever it is she's an offering to will eat her. She guesses it depends how quickly the water reaches neck level, and for how long it stays there. Either way, it won't be pretty.

Defeated, she slumps backward and closes her eyes. In her mind, she tries to go somewhere else. Washington. She conjures the scent of pine and sea salt, the sound of waves slapping rocky shores, the hum of public buses. And just when she has it, something... *slurps.*

Janie keeps her eyes squeezed shut, imagining some Cthulhu-like creature rising from the muddy lake bed, tentacles writhing, rows of teeth gnashing, ready to gobble her up and fulfill the unholy contract. There's another *slurp*, closer now. Janie's stomach twists. Her fingers tremble.

"Hey," a voice says.

Janie's eyes snap open, lashes dripping rainwater. A man is standing there, slurping a Sonic Route 44 like he's at a backyard barbeque and not the bottom of a flooding lake. He's wearing cargo shorts and a Pabst Blue Ribbon t-shirt. The man takes another loud, lingering drink.

"Who're you?" she sputters through the rain. A small part of her hopes this stranger is here to save her, but a bigger part knows better than to hope.

The man studies her, gnawing absently at the red straw in his drink. His eyes are the color of a brewing storm.

"I'm the Lake God," he says finally. If Janie weren't tethered to a piece of wood at the bottom of the lake, she wouldn't believe for a second that this guy is god of anything; he looks like he works at a bait shop. But she *is* tethered to a piece of wood at the bottom of the lake, so she figures he's probably telling the truth.

"I'm the offering," Janie replies.

Rain is still pouring violently from the sky. Every drop that hits Janie's skin feels like a shot from a pellet gun. The Lake God takes another long drink and shoves his free hand in his pocket.

"Yeah," he sighs. "Sure looks like it."

Janie says nothing. Her wrists feel like the skin's been rubbed off them and her eyes sting from the rain. The only thing keeping her from collapsing into a puddle is the rope tethering her to the beam. She doesn't want to die for this shithole town, and she *definitely* doesn't want to play human sacrifice to a god that can't even muster some goddamn enthusiasm about it.

The Lake God steps closer, still chewing on his straw. He smells like soil and pond scum, like algae washed ashore and left to rot in the sun.

"So, what's a young thing like you doing here?" he asks. "Thought it'd be one of the older ones. You know, for efficiency's sake." The Lake God shakes his head like he can't believe it.

"I was going to leave," Janie says. "I was moving to Seattle for school next month. I was going to be a hydrologist." She doesn't know why she keeps rambling. Maybe she's having one of those moments that people sometimes have right before they die, when they're compelled to confess their darkest secrets and dearest wishes.

"That's a damn shame. Seattle's a real nice place. Best cup of coffee I've ever had."

"Well, too bad I won't have a chance to try it," Janie says dryly.

The Lake God asks for her name. She tells him. *Janie Rivas. Nice to meet you.* She imagines she's at freshman orientation, introducing herself to her class, instead of at the bottom of a lake, introducing herself to a reluctant God.

"Well, listen, Janie. This is mighty awkward, but this whole—" the Lake God gestures at her bindings "—*human sacrifice* business isn't much to my taste anymore."

The sky is a dark, miasmic gray. The rain is falling so hard and fast that Janie can barely keep her eyes open. Her clothes are heavy and cold on her slick skin.

"Then why's this the first time it's rained in five years?" Janie asks, panting.

A shadow, like a storm cloud, passes over the Lake God's face. A great burst of lightning forks across the sky and a surge of rainfall pours down, heavy as the slap of an ocean wave. The Lake God stands immovable at the bottom of the lake, now the eye of a hurricane. Janie cries out. The water is rising, reaching up like the hands of the dead beckoning for her to come down and join them. And then, as quickly as it started, the rain stops. The wind holds its breath. The water lapping at Janie's knees goes still. The Lake God looks at her with eyes the color of a starless sky. He chews on his straw some more, thoughtfully. His Pabst Blue Ribbon shirt is curiously dry.

"Janie," he says finally, "How 'bout you and I talk this over some place where you aren't in imminent peril of drowning?"

"Sounds swell," says Janie.

The Lake God, inexplicably, drives an old Ford Bronco, and with it, he drives them to a gas station halfway between Sunrise Beach and the next ghost town. The rain has stopped and the air smells strangely of damp hot dogs. All but one gas pump are covered with faded yellow bags that says, "Out of Order." The Lake God buys them each a clownishly large soda and they sit outside on the curb, talking for a long time.

"So, you've been on vacation for five years?" Janie asks.

"Well," he says, "I was Lake God for a lot longer than that." Even gods, it seems, tire eventually. But the Lake God assures Janie that he took precautions. Or, at least, he thought he did. His cousin from

Lake Tahoe was supposed to check in on the place every so often. "Guess this is why they say not to mix family and business," he grumbles.

"What now?" Janie asks. Part of her hopes he'll smite the town of Sunrise Beach with a terrible flood, a freak superstorm the likes of which the world has never seen. A larger part just wants to forget this nasty business, order a large pizza, and take a long, hot shower.

"Well," says the Lake God. "I s'pose I could stick around to take care of the lake, but then what if someone gets it in their head to offer up another poor soul next time there's a drought?"

"If you were around to take care of the lake, there wouldn't be another drought," Janie points out.

The Lake God stabs his straw further into his drink, muddling the crushed ice at the bottom. Above them, the clouds swirl, tinged the same stormy gray as his eyes.

"I never liked being tied down." He says the words with a strange sort of resignation, like he's been tasked with the cosmic equivalent of cleaning the toilet.

They sit in silence, watching the clouds brew dark storms in their underbellies. A gust of wind swirls through the parking lot, kicking up puffs of dirt.

Janie sighs. She doesn't miss the tourists, but she sure does hate to see the place she grew up gone to shit. That's why she decided to go to Seattle to become a hydrologist in the first place. She'd find untapped groundwater, or engineer some genius irrigation system to restore the lake. But now... if she'd known it was as easy as being a Lake God, she might've checked what the course load for that particular field of study looked like.

"What if someone else took care of the lake? Someone other than your cousin, I mean," Janie says.

The Lake God rubs his chin. Overhead, the clouds still. "Well now, Janie," he says. "Isn't that an idea?"

When Janie shows back up in town later that day, the people of Sunrise Beach give her a wide berth. If it weren't raining, they'd probably drag her back down to the bottom of the lake, but it *is* raining, so they let her stay. Still, no one knows quite what to say to her. Some of the townspeople feel guilty, but for most of them, it's just awkward. Yeah, it's great that the Lake God spared her, but does she have to rub it in their faces? A few people work up the courage to ask questions.

"What happened down there, Janie?"

"Did you see him?"

"What did he say?"

Whenever these questions come, Janie just shrugs. She keeps to herself. She watches a lot of Netflix and, occasionally, goes for a swim in the lake. When it's not raining, that is.

There are whispers that maybe the Lake God didn't spare Janie. Maybe she just made a deal with him. The good people of Sunrise Beach are afraid. On the day Janie leaves for Seattle, Myrna Fairway and Lou Conaway of the Sunrise Beach City Council resign, and Mayor Cobb skips town entirely. The people burn down the City Hall as their own kind of offering and hope that's the end of it. No one is harmed, and the citizens of Sunrise Beach are steadfast in their silence about what exactly happened and *who* is responsible.

Janie, of course, won't hear about this until months later, when she returns to Sunrise Beach over fall break, accompanied by a man that smells of wet soil and algae. In Washington, Janie's learned of drainage-basin management and agricultural water balance and flood forecasting. She's pleased to find that, after all that, summoning rains comes quite naturally.

After graduation, the man that was once the Lake God claps her on the back as they say their farewells. When Janie asks where he plans to go, he says, "Somewhere without any damn lakes, that's for sure!"

When Janie returns to Sunrise Beach for good, the tourists return as well, filling every restaurant and dive bar and pool hall. The townspeople still don't know what to say to Janie, or whether they should say anything at all. At first, they're too afraid to let their children splash in puddles, let alone swim in the lake. But, after five years of steady rain, their fears grow dull and they grow bored, so they pull the tarps off their fishing boats. They pack their coolers with beer and hard seltzers. The cautious ones buy their children life jackets. They convince themselves that if one of them had been chosen as the offering, Janie would've stood in the crowd, watching and waiting and saying nothing, just like they did.

Janie lets the townsfolk think what they will. Her blood has long since turned to water, and with it, any rage she felt ebbed away like a wave receding from the shore.

See Caite Sajwaj's story "Dry Season" online at Metaphorosis.
If you liked it, leave a comment. Authors love that!
Remember to subscribe to our e-mail updates so you'll know when new stories are posted.

About the story

When I started writing "Dry Season", the one thing I knew for sure was that it'd be set in Lake of the Ozarks during a very extended drought. The plot only started to develop during the pandemic, when tourism completely dried up. For a place like Sunrise Beach, which is so small it's technically a village and has an economy that relies almost completely on tourism, that was devastating. When things get that dire, people often appeal to their deity of choice. And, there it was: the inciting incident of the story.

Next came the characters, and the rest of the story is more theirs than mine.

First, the people of Sunrise Beach, who are presented as a sort of collective consciousness. This was inspired by the chorus of the Maids in Margaret Atwood's "The Penelopiad" (though the townsfolk of Sunrise Beach are certainly guilty where the Maids were not). It's also an unintended reference to groupthink—surprise!

The Lake God, was originally intended to be this sort of primordial, eldritch beast. In his present form, he's more a distillation of Lake of the Ozarks given human form. That decision was completely spontaneous. Honestly, it was less a decision and more, "Well, there he is." His character is, rather unexpectedly, very precious to me, and I hope you all enjoy him.

Now, Janie, is very different than any protagonist I've ever written in that we aren't privy to many of her thoughts. She's really a reflection of my own somewhat complicated relationship with being from a rural town. Clearly, she both loves and loathes Sunrise Beach, and, like many of us that both love and loathe our hometowns, she's developed a bit of a savior complex about it. Hey, if she ends up unhappy in her new role, she can always find someone else to take over, right?

A question for the author

Q: Do you have a garden? Have you ever grown your own food?

A: I'm what you might call "in between" gardens right now. We recently moved and I was only able to bring along some herbs and two potted tomato plants. Now, I'm in the process of planning a new garden that will make much better use of space and produce a lot more food. My hope is that we'll be able to grow enough food to share with our neighbors and local food pantry. We'll plant a flower garden to feed our pollinator friends too, of course!

About the author

Caite Sajwaj writes ghost stories and tall tales inspired by the urban fringe areas of the Midwest. When not writing, she enjoys gardening, craft cocktails, and befriending the neighborhood crows. She lives in Lawrence, Kansas, with her husband and their rescue dog, Josie.

caitesajwaj.com, @CaiteSajwaj

Stand or Fall

David Whitmarsh

Ilyas Bardakci was dead, but he hadn't stopped breathing, hadn't stopped moving, hadn't stopped thinking. He had no chance, no hope, no idea where in the void of interstellar space his ship had emerged. The radiation pulse from the nuke that had torn through his flesh had burned through half the ship's systems. That was the price he'd paid for hesitating. Wavering between solidarity and vengeance, he'd left it too late and jumped blind.

The reactor was down. Backup power was enough to keep the air pumping, the lights on, and the remaining instruments running, at least for a few hours. If life support lasted long enough, the radiation sickness would certainly kill him, but he wasn't dead yet, unlike those he'd left behind. Thinking of them fed the rage and the rage beat down the rising nausea. His fingers danced over the controls. Telescopes and sensors on the hull of the tiny vessel twisted on their mounts, searching for bearings of the brightest stars. Tentative spectral matches scrolled up the display: Sirius, Muphrid, Denebola. Calculations converged on an answer: he was twenty-eight light-years from the Muphrid system where he'd started.

For Ilyas, the jump had happened in the blink of an eye, but during that timeless instant twenty-eight years had elapsed. Twenty-eight years since everyone and everything he had known had perished. The habitats, stations, planet-side cities, a hundred and forty million people. All gone. Twenty-eight light-years behind him, twenty-eight years in the past. Celeste had been right: fighting was futile, and he had lost her because of his refusal to listen.

With no reactor, he could jump again only as far as the residual charge in the drive allowed. A search of the almanac revealed the colony closest to his crippled vessel: GJ430.1, HIP 56238, a star so insignificant it was nameless, known only by numbers from ancient catalogues; so dim it was barely a star at all. No major planets, two balls of rock smaller than Earth's moon, and a meagre smattering of asteroids, yet people lived there, and it was less than three light-years from his current position.

In the placid emptiness of the interstellar void he had time to check the calculations. With the autopilot dead, he had to point the vessel by hand and eye towards his target and set the displacement to the required range.

Another instant, another three years. His telescope found the single habitat cylinder, Thurlina, twenty kilometres long, four in diameter, turning its slow dance close around the dim red star. The docking complex at the sunlit axis held a handful of kinetic in-system tugs and freighters, nothing with interstellar capability. Population seven hundred thousand according to the almanac, a pacific society, friendly, welcoming, but a cultural and industrial backwater. The almanac was sixty years out of date.

His hand, beginning to blister from the radiation burns, lifted the cover from the mayday alarm. He passed out before he could press it.

Weight pressed him down on a soft bed. Muted footsteps paced around his dreams.

Celeste.

No. Celeste had given up the fight long ago. The soft footsteps faded and he slid from delirium to darkness.

A soft bed, a softly-lit windowless room. Ilyas tried to speak, but his throat was dry. He raised his arm to test the strength of the gravity that held him down, but learned only his own weakness. Wires snaked out from under the bedclothes to the monitors by the bedside. Thin tubes red with blood penetrated the pale blotchy skin of his arm.

"Water," he mumbled, and blacked out again.

Grey eyes peered at him from above the mask, wisps of ash-blond hair escaping from the edge of the cap.

"Awake, hey?" A female voice. "You're better off sleeping through this part." She turned from him and her arms moved but he couldn't see what her hands were doing. A few clicks, a beep. The room receded and his eyelids closed of their own accord. Celeste waited for him, sitting out on the balcony of their small apartment, the light of the sun-tube bright on her bare arms.

She looked up from the book she was reading. "How did it go? Did you save anyone?"

No. They're all dead, he tried to answer, but his mouth was too dry.

Celeste laid down the book. "But you got away. You're alive. Don't waste that." She raised her right hand to stroke his cheek, red blood dripping from the gash along her wrist. "I'm sorry, sweetheart."

Sorry for what she had done, or for what he had? Ilyas couldn't tell.

"Stand or Fall! Stand or Fall!" Ilyas had shouted with the rest of them as they stood in the great hall. On the giant screen above the stage, they cheered as the demolition charges rippled through the evacuation fleet. They cheered again when the image of the expanding cloud of debris was replaced by Marshal Petro's stern face.

"How do you feel today, Ilyas?" The same grey eyes, the same ash-blond hair, but no cap, no mask. Young, pretty, like the daughter he'd never had. Her hair was short, neat. No cosmetics, no jewellery except a thin chain around her neck that hung down beneath her blouse.

"Thirsty," he croaked.

She held the cup with one hand and raised his head with the other while he grasped the straw between his lips. Cold water flooded his mouth, the sweetest thing he had ever tasted.

"Slowly," she said. "Not too much."

He swallowed and relaxed to allow his head to be lowered back to the pillow. "How long?"

"You've been here three weeks. A tug pulled you in to the dock after your jump triggered the sensors."

"Thank the crew for me."

"No crew. Automated. We've a lot of automation in Thurlina." She smiled like it was a joke. "When you're a little stronger you'll see. For now you need to rest, and you are not my only patient."

On her way out she paused to look back at him. "I'm Mila. Mila Kraft." The door closed and her soft footsteps faded to silence. Silence that drew on and on until Ilyas fell asleep again.

For a few minutes, the ablative dust clouds had done their job. The Enemy's hypervelocity projectiles blasted to plasma as they collided with the fine grains, but the shock waves carved openings in the clouds faster than they could be replenished. For years, the people of Muphrid had worked to build those defences but they brought only minutes of respite. The projectiles, simple fragments of iron each weighing a few grams but travelling close to the speed of light, tore into the orbital habitats, stations, and cities, each piece with the energy of a small nuclear device. Hundreds of them, thousands, millions.

Ilyas and his squadron waited to defend against the second wave of the attack. By the time it came they were defending expanding clouds of dust and debris and craters glowing red.

Ilyas lay wide awake in the soft bed in the softly lit room. A faint hissing and burbling from the machine pumping his blood had been the only sound since the gentle machine that washed and wiped and dressed him had left the room with motors whirring. That had been ten minutes ago, or an hour, or two. He searched for his anger, but it was weak, as he was.

Footsteps approached, the door opened. Dr Mila Kraft entered with her sad smile. A trolley followed her in on silent wheels.

"Good morning, Ilyas."

"Doctor."

She raised the head of the bed so he sat upright and summoned a machine from the corner of the room, one with jointed cermel arms and fine grippers. The hissing and burbling of the blood pump faded out.

"This may sting a little." She watched as the machine disconnected the blood-filled tubes from his arm. Gentle pressure, and the thick needles were withdrawn, a dressing applied. A dull ache, nothing more.

She lifted the cover from the trolley that had followed her in. A rich spicy smell filled the room. His mouth watered, his stomach tightened painfully.

"You came from Muphrid," she said as she lifted the tray from the trolley. "The mechs pulled the log from your vessel."

"Yes."

"We picked up the last transmission from Muphrid a little while before you arrived. I'm so sorry." She laid the tray across his lap. He picked up the spoon and dipped it into the dark orange liquid. "Take it slow. The treatment you've had has been... intensive. It'll take time for your system to settle down."

"OK." His hand shook as he raised the spoon.

"Can you manage?"

"Think so." Warm, thick, flavours of coriander and cumin and other spices unfamiliar. Ilyas closed his eyes and absorbed the taste, the texture.

"Your vessel wasn't designed for interstellar flight."

It was a statement, not a question. The spoon paused on its way back to the bowl. "A weapons control platform. The drive was originally from a long-range scoutship, adapted for multiple short jumps on a single charge. I was trying to make a sub-second jump, a hundred thousand kilometres to escape a missile. It detonated early and the radiation scrambled my flight controls. I jumped nearly thirty light-years."

"I'm sorry," she said. "I shouldn't distract you. Eat."

When the bowl was empty she placed the tray back on the trolley and sent it away. As it left the room a chair rolled in to take its place.

"Swing your legs out." She took his upper arm and elbow and eased him to a standing position. His legs shook as she turned and lowered him into the chair. Hard to judge in his weakened state but the spin of the habitat gave a gravity close to standard. Even so, she supported him and lowered him into the chair with practised ease.

She walked beside his chair along the long echoing corridor. Ilyas squinted against the bright light from the window at the end.

"You really believed you could hold off the Enemy at Muphrid?"

"We did."

"Even after what happened to the Sol system, to Earth?"

"A lack of commitment, Marshal Petro said. Everywhere before us put more effort into running away than trying to fight. No one ran from Muphrid."

"Why not?"

"We didn't let them." Ten years of martial law after Petro seized power, all the considerable industrial capacity of the Muphrid system had been dedicated to defence. No effort wasted on evacuation ships. Those under construction or not yet departed had been destroyed as a demonstration of resolve. They'd taken the drives out first, though. The scoutship drives went into weapons control platforms like Ilyas's ship, the colony ship drives into the rail-gun and missile batteries. Except one; Marshal Petro had kept one of those drives for his own use: a yacht, mobile presidential palace, centre of government, military headquarters.

A means of escape.

Now the anger rose. Two hundred thousand people could have escaped on the evacuation fleet. Two hundred thousand out of a hundred and forty million. Ilyas's anger was not directed at the Enemy, the Enemy was impersonal, implacable, like the tides that ripped apart a sun as it spiralled into a neutron star. No one knew where the Enemy came from or why they sought the extinction of the human species. A plague of machines spreading from star to star killing everyone, destroying everything, they were like a force of nature. Anger at them was pointless.

His anger, his hatred, he held solely for Marshal Petro, who had misled him, misled all of them, before finally betraying them. Through all the years since the evacuation fleet was blown up Ilyas had convinced himself it had been the right thing to do. He had had to believe it, had to believe that Celeste had been wrong to do as she did. "Stand or fall," he muttered through clenched teeth.

The window at the end of the corridor looked out onto the townscape of Thurlina, lengthways along the cylindrical habitat, a jumble of white-walled buildings and narrow streets broken up with small greens, broad parklands, trees. To right and left the ground curved up, fading into the blue-grey of a sunlit haze. Along the axis high above, the sun-tube glared with the bright yellow-white of Earth's sun. Familiar yet strange. His own home habitat was twice the size, with taller buildings, ziggurat shaped apartment blocks reaching up towards the sun-tube. Some of the larger buildings here in Thurlina had one or more narrow towers or pointed spires, each bearing on its wall or pinnacle the cross and crescent symbol of the Syntheist faith.

"I came from Muphrid." Ilyas looked up at Mila. "We followed the Humanist Covenant."

She stood still beside him, unperturbed by his observation. "Don't be concerned, Ilyas. Our faith isn't like some sects. Church and Covenant have lived in harmony in Thurlina since the colony was founded."

A small bird with a yellow breast, shades of delicate blue on the wings and head, and a dark band across the eyes sang in the high branches of a tree some metres from the window. It stood out sharply against the green leaves. Nothing else moved. Thurlina was home to seven hundred thousand people, according to his almanac, but the almanac was sixty years out of date. There had been no interstellar ships in the docks when he arrived, no way for anyone to escape when the Enemy reached here.

"My ship was damaged," he said, "but the drive was intact." A single-seater, someone in Thurlina was bound to claim it for themselves, to get away before the Enemy came here, too.

"The mechs are doing what they do when they find something broken. They're fixing it."

"What will happen to it?"

She touched her hand to his shoulder. "You can leave when it's ready, when you're well enough."

The lift took them down to the ground floor, and the chair rolled across a wide entrance lobby: white walls, shining floor, the light of the sun-tube pouring in through tall glass windows. No one stood behind the reception desk, no one sat in the low couches of the waiting area. Nothing moved except a small spider mech working its way across the expanse of glass, cleaning away unseen dirt. Glass doors slid silently aside to allow them into the grassed grounds around the hospital. Ilyas had not seen so much green space in over a decade, since before they'd built the flight training facility over his local park, the same facility where he had enlisted. Ilyas's chair rolled beside Mila along the path and round the side of the building to a row of modest single-storey houses. The light was fading, the glare of the sun-tube diminishing, the shadowy patchwork of streets and buildings becoming visible overhead on the far side of the cylinder.

"This is yours." Mila led him up a path to the third door. "Kitchen, bedroom, living area. There's a gym at the back. You can cook for yourself or order in. Eat and drink small amounts, often, until your stomach is used to food again. Gentle exercise; just stand and sit a few times today. You'll soon get your strength back."

An aurocular lay on the living room table. She picked it up and handed it to him. "Anything you need, just ask, or call me. I'll be back in a couple of hours to check on you."

The aurocular was a commonplace design, hooking over the ears and resting on the brow. The earpieces slipped into place and the lasers projected their image into his eyes. A few blinks, a few words and he was looking at a 3D projection of what had once been settled space, a rough globe of stars centred on Sol. Nu Phoenicis, the first to fall to the Enemy, lay at the surface on one side. Zosma almost diametrically opposite. Most of the stars shone as white dots. Those that had been settled, but now known to be lost to the Enemy, were red. Green denoted those where humanity still survived — doubtless some of those had fallen, but news travelled slowly on starships or laser beams, percolating through settled space at the speed of light. The globe, a hundred light-years across, was speckled with red. Green stars clustered in a lens-shaped region roughly centred on the axis between Sol and Zosma.

Ilyas zoomed in on the region around this system, GJ430.1. Muphrid glowed red, having fallen thirty years before. The Enemy's usual pattern would have them consolidate their position in one system for between one and five years, rebuilding their arsenal to assault the next, jumping at light speed. Years yet before they would reach here from Muphrid, but Muphrid was not the nearest red star. Ilyas drilled down into the details of Gliese 3649, a small research station seven years away: contact had been lost two years before.

It might be ten years before the Enemy arrived from Muphrid. It could be tomorrow if they came from Gliese 3649.

On his own two feet, Ilyas made it into the kitchen and stood, legs shaking, elbows on the countertop to take his weight, while he waited for a prepared concoction of pasta, tomato, and mycoprotein to heat through. After the meal he shuffled into the hallway and down to the bathroom. The absence of hair when he unzipped caught him by surprise. The radiation, or the treatment. He ran his hand over his scalp — a fine stiff fuzz rippled beneath his fingers. A look in the mirror revealed a gaunt face with skin raw pink stretched tight and a uniform dark shadow of emerging hair on his scalp. His fingers explored the sharp boundary at the temple where the receding edge had formerly given him a pronounced widow's peak.

Raised voices outside dragged him from his reflection. He stumbled out from the bathroom to the front door and grasped a handrail for support. Just outside the next dwelling, a woman sat in a wheelchair. Hair short and white, face filled with deep creases. Her hand curled claw-like on the arm of the chair. Mila Kraft crouched facing her, speaking too softly to hear.

"No! Leave me alone! Sinner!" the old woman shouted. Her chair wheeled around and carried her into her house. Mila stood, facing the door for a moment, then turned and walked away.

Another of Mila's patients. Ilyas made his way indoors and returned to the lounge, to the aurocular, to the globe of green and red dots. Amongst the green, the most populous system was Denebola. A system rich with natural resources and a mature industrial base eighteen years from Thurlina. The latest news from Denebola was of a construction programme for a fleet of colony ships to travel a thousand light years or more into the beyond, to find a new home far from settled space, far from the Enemy.

No guarantees. No one knew where the Enemy came from. They might be anywhere out there, or they might continue their expansion to reach the refugees in a thousand years. But to be lucky, you have to survive, to stay in the game until the next roll of the dice.

Nearer than Denebola lay Zosma, less than seven years away. Less well developed but with settlements on one of a pair of binary planets and in the space around. A cultural melange of evacuees from throughout settled space. It was questionable whether they had the capacity to build the drives for a large colony ship, like the drive in Marshal Petro's yacht, but the hull, the robotics and industrial base for a new colony, those were easy to build. If Petro had gone there, he could bargain with them for the resources to rebuild his yacht into a colony ship. He might save a thousand people, maybe more. At Muphrid they might have saved two hundred thousand. Ilyas's anger seethed

Denebola and Zosma were the two systems to which Petro might have fled. Others were too small, too hostile, or too close to the curving plane of the Enemy's advance. If Ilyas followed Petro to Zosma, he would only be three years behind him; Thurlina lay almost on the straight-line route from Muphrid. Denebola was closer to Muphrid than Thurlina was. By the time Ilyas could reach Denebola it would be nearly fifty years since the fall of Muphrid, thirty since Petro could have arrived there, and probably at least ten since it was overrun by the Enemy

Ilyas's anger congealed to cold purpose. He would go to Zosma, three years behind Petro, find him and exact the justice he deserved. He would require luck, that Petro would not have already completed his colony ship and escaped to the beyond, that Ilyas could get close enough to him to take his revenge, but luck had favoured Ilyas so far: the jump from Muphrid had landed him close to Thurlina, Mila Kraft had saved his life, and his ship would be returned to him. Luck had favoured Ilyas Bardakci, as long as he could avoid thinking about what he had lost.

A brief spell in the gym, every machine set to the lightest of the stone weights on their cords, then Ilyas was hungry again, ravenous. A knock at the door interrupted him half-way through his second plate of assorted vegetables with a slab of some cultured protein.

Mila's brow furrowed when he opened the door, still chewing "Don't overdo it, Ilyas, you'll make yourself sick."

She sat him down in the lounge, strapped a monitor on his arm and slipped an aurocular on her brow to read it. Her eyes were drawn to the space over the coffee table where his virtual projection of the star map hung.

"They'll be here soon," he said. "The Enemy."

"I know." She lowered her eyes. "Your pulse, blood pressure are good. You must be feeling a little stronger already. I should explain the treatment you've received."

"My almanac said seven hundred thousand people lived here, but that was sixty years ago. How many are there now?"

"Three."

"Three hundred thousand?"

"No." She peered at him from under the brow of the aurocular. "Three. Including you."

Ilyas stared in silence at her waiting eyer, taking it in. Seven hundred thousand.

"How?"

"A hundred years ago we heard of the loss of Nu Phoenicis. A far away tragedy, all we could do was hold those who suffered and died in our prayers. Then as the years went by and more systems fell, the church council realised that one day they would reach us here. The council resolved that when they did, there should be no one for them to kill." She slipped her aurocular off. "Sixty years ago, we stopped having children."

"Many families at Muphrid did have children. They had faith in Marshal Petro. They had hope for the future."

"Not you?"

Ilyas's eyes ranged unseeing from Mila, to the living room window, to his own hands clasped in his lap. "I had faith, but Celeste, my wife, she wouldn't have children unless we could leave. Then... I lost her."

"Lost her?"

Ten years, and the pain of it was still so sharp he couldn't talk about it.

"Marshal Petro never asked the children at Muphrid whether we should stand and fight." He raised his head and met Mila's eyes. "You stopped having children sixty years ago? There should be tens, hundreds of thousands of people still here."

"This system is poor in resources. The population long ago reached the limit that we could support, so there were few children. Afterwards, we stripped the system bare of metals to build what ships we could, scavenged from those we already had and sent them out to the beyond to find a new life. We were able to build enough to send away everyone with a subjective age under fifty. The rest have all lived out their lives in peace here. Only Isolde is left."

Isolde. His neighbour. "And you. How long since you came back?"

"Back? I've never been away."

"You're young. You said there were no children born in the last sixty years. I assumed you'd gained years from relativity."

A half-smile, a nod of understanding. "Almost no children. Biology is hard to tame, Ilyas. Accidents happen. I *was* born after the last ship left."

Birds were singing with the brightening of the sun-tube when Ilyas woke from a deep, dreamless sleep. His muscles sang with a gentle tension and his joints tingled with the need to move. He pulled the cover aside and briskly stood, marched into the bathroom, urinated, washed. The mirror showed him a face thin rather than gaunt, a body taut and slender rather than famished. That thought awakened his appetite and he stepped smartly around the wheelchair in the hallway, heading for the kitchen.

Bread, hummus, dried fruits, and a crunchy biscuit of insect protein took the edge off enough for the desire to move, walk, run, jump, shout to override his hunger.

Ilyas stepped out of his front door and ran. He ran along the path that led back around to the front of the hospital building and out of the grounds, past stone pillars and into a maze of narrow winding streets. On either hand, stone walls with closed doors and vacant windows. On corners, plate glass of cafés, shops, hairdressers, each one pristine, shining, ready to greet its next customer. Looking back the way he had come, the five-storey facade of the hospital dominated the houses. Behind it, the slope of the habitat's end cap rose up, a patchwork of greens and browns cut through with spiral paths, fading into a white haze as it curved to vertical.

Street after street looped in long curves to new streets, all different but all the same, until one bend opened up onto a wide park. Rabbits grazed on grassland dotted with trees and cut by a lake that curved gently around the habitat's circumference. In the middle of a low, arching, wooden bridge over the lake Ilyas stopped, gasping for breath. Sweat ran down his face and stung his eyes. The scene around him darkened. His eyes filled with thickening shadows and his legs buckled beneath him.

Before the lockdown, Celeste had wanted them to flee Muphrid, to try and secure a place on a departing ship, any ship, going anywhere.

"Treat the world as it is!" she'd shouted, "You're deluding yourself, Ilyas, you can't fight the Enemy!"

Ilyas expected her to leave him the day he went to the great hall to cheer on the demolition of the evacuation fleet. She did, in her own way. He returned to a silent apartment, to her naked form lying motionless in a bath of crimson water. When he had reached for her hand he sliced open his own palm on the shard of glass she held, his blood mingling with hers.

"Stand or fall," he murmured.

"What was that, Ilyas?" Mila Kraft was sitting by his bedside.

"What happened?"

"You fainted. I did tell you not to overdo it." She held out a glass of pale liquid. "Drink this."

He shuffled up the bed to sit upright, took the glass, and drank. Cool, sweet. "I felt so... alive."

She took the empty glass from him. "How old are you, Ilyas?"

"I was born twenty-five eighty CE, eighty-nine years ago, and I've lived about fifty-seven of those." Thirty-two years in all spent in the timeless instants of light-speed travel, almost all of that in the journey from Muphrid.

She leaned forward, elbows on knees and reached out to take his hand. She held it palm uppermost. The scar that had crossed his palm was gone.

"You are eighty-nine elapsed years old, fifty-seven subjective. You were close to death when you came here, Ilyas. I don't know how much radiation you'd received, but many times a fatal dose."

"I guess I'll need to worry about cancers..."

"No, you won't. Didn't your almanac tell you about Thurlina's specialisation in medical science? I did a full-body tissue regeneration. You've lost a lot of weight with flushing out the dead and damaged cells but you now have a biological age of twenty-five."

The lost scar, restored sharpness of vision. The taut flesh, the once-receding hair now regrowing. Mila sat, still holding his hand in hers, her hand and his both with clear, unblemished skin.

"What you said about your birth being an accident. Was that true, or are you really…"

She let go the hand. "True enough. I'm older than I look, but not that old. I was born after the last starship left. As the youngest, I would have to care for the last ones, so I trained as a doctor and I gave myself the treatments that the older generation denied themselves. The same as I had to give you to save your life."

"So, I could live another eighty years, subjective?"

"One step at a time, Ilyas. Let's get you well, first."

She gave him an exercise programme and dietary advice and left him with strict instructions not to exceed the boundaries she'd laid down.

"Walk before you run," she said. "Tomorrow we'll go for a gentle walk."

After a shower and another light meal, Ilyas rested. In the evening, as the sun-tube dimmed, he ventured out to take the short stroll that Mila's programme allowed him.

"Are you another one?" A quavering voice called out from the shadowed porch of the adjacent house.

Ilyas ambled up the path and crouched down before the seated figure. "Another what, Isolde?" She was old, wrinkles joined to creases and wrapped into folds of sagging skin beneath thin, curled hair. A straggle of stiff grey hairs struggled from her upper lip.

"Damned impertinence. Using my name without giving one in return."

"Ilyas." He offered his hand.

Isolde *harrumphed*, flicked the joystick, and her chair wheeled around and into her house.

"The mechs have some questions about your ship." The light of the sun-tube sparkled on the lake as they walked, Mila's hand on Ilyas's arm to steady him.

"What kind of questions?"

"They'd like to replace some of the damaged metal components with composites. Metals are scarce here."

"That's OK."

They walked a dozen paces in silence.

"There's something else," Mila said. She stopped and turned to face him. "They said there was a range limiter. It was restricted to jumps no more than a light-day, but it had been bypassed."

Ilyas fixed his gaze on the trees on the lake's far shore.

"Treat the world as it is, Ilyas, not how you wish it were. That applies to your own self as much as the world about you. To move on, to heal, you have to reconcile yourself to what happened. Your escape from Muphrid wasn't an accident, was it?"

A dozen heartbeats, two long breaths Ilyas kept his eyes on the trees. "Ten years before the Enemy came to Muphrid, Marshal Petro ordered the destruction of the evacuation fleet. There would be no way out for any of us. I took my place in the squadron thinking that if Petro were wrong, I'd die with everyone else when the Enemy came." One more deep breath and he looked Mila in eyes. "A short while before the end, a colleague, an engineer, told me about the limiter and how to bypass it. All the ships built on drives salvaged from the evacuation fleet had them except Marshal Petro's yacht. If the defence failed, he could get away, he and his family. We were *all* supposed to stay. Stand or fall, victory or death."

Ilyas turned away and folded his arms. "When I found out about Petro's yacht, I swore he would pay if the defence failed. I don't know that he got away, but if he did, I intend to find him."

Petro must have gone to Zosma. At Zosma he would have had leverage, a starship drive that could power a colony ship. At Denebola, he would have been one more desperate refugee.

She took his arm again and they walked on in silence. They crossed the bridge over the lake and sat at one of a dozen empty tables outside a cafe. A mech served them fresh salad with a pale oily fish.

"How long could this last?" he asked. "If the Enemy didn't come."

"Who knows? The habitat shell would last indefinitely. The mechs repair and replace themselves; everything is recycled."

"But the Enemy will come."

She didn't answer.

"What will you do, you and Isolde?"

She looked at him. "We always knew some us might be alive when the Enemy came. We have implants. When the sensors detect the Enemy's approach, that will trigger the implants and release a drug."

In every system, the attack took the same form. The first thing the sensors would detect would be the gravity waves as the Enemy's forces jumped to the system's outer reaches. Within hours, the hail of hypervelocity projectiles would shatter or vaporise anything fixed, or too big to move quickly. Finally, the missiles would come, jumping into the inner system to seek and destroy anything that remained and mop up survivors. Ilyas's mission had been to direct the rail guns to defend against the missiles, but just as the hail of hypervelocity projectiles had overwhelmed the protective shields of dust, so the missiles had kept coming and coming. Too many, too fast for the defences.

"My wife, Celeste, she took her own life after the evacuation fleet was destroyed."

"I can understand that." Mila reached out to rest her hand on his. "But our faith doesn't allow us to intentionally take a life, even our own. The implant releases a sedative so we'll be asleep when the Enemy strikes."

"My ship, if the mechs stripped out the sensors, the weapons control systems, boosted the life support, they might make room for two."

She closed her eyes and raised her face to the sky. "I used to dream of what I would do if I were away from here. The life I could lead... friends... lovers... children."

She drew her hand away. "All my life I've known I would be here until the end, caring for my elders. I can't change now. I can't leave Isolde."

"Nineteen days." Ilyas set his empty wine glass down. "Why do you have a feast every nineteen days?"

Mila raised and tilted the bottle towards him. He nodded and she poured. "Syntheism is a fusion of all the old religions. The nineteen-day feast is a tradition we inherited from the Bahá'i."

Isolde, sat hunched in her chair, but with a grin on her face and a sparkle in her eyes. "Itself a mongrel faith," she cackled.

"And the Covenant is just Buddhism without spirituality." Mila retorted.

That set Isolde laughing again, and Mila joined her. They were both in their finery. Isolde wore a fine quilted jacked in dark greens and maroons, embroidered in gold thread. Gold, here where metals of any kind were more precious than anywhere. Gold too, the cross and crescent pendant that hung from Mila's neck, framed by her low-cut dress.

"Why 'sinners', Isolde?" Ilyas took a sip from his glass. "What sin have we committed?"

Mila grinned and rolled her eyes.

Isolde pointed her crooked finger at Mila, then Ilyas. "Look at you both, in the full flush of youth. What of the penance!"

"Penance?"

Mila pushed her plate away. "A penance for our hubris. We have affronted God and his prophets with our desire for eternal youth, and so we should allow ourselves to grow old and die a natural death before the Enemy comes. But Isolde, that oath was made before I was born. I'm not bound by the promises of my elders."

"Bah! That's Covenant talk. You were raised in the faith."

"And you were raised in the Covenant. Isolde. Atheists."

"*Atheist* defines us by what we are not," Ilyas said, catching Isolde's eye. "What we *are* is humanists," they chorused.

"But Isolde," Ilyas continued. "you're Covenant, yet you still followed the faith's edict to grow old?"

Isolde paused, the laughter fell from her eyes. "You and I both know that gods are fairy tales for the credulous, young man, but solidarity with your community is an essential part of humanity. How would I have felt if I'd stayed young and beautiful while my friends and neighbours all withered with age?"

Ilyas nodded. "Covenant solidarity played a big part for us at Muphrid."

Isolde's hand banged the table with surprising ferocity. "Yet you forgot the Covenant's first precept! *Treat the world as it is, not as you wish it were!*" Her needle-sharp eyes bored into Ilyas. "Year after year I saw the news feeds coming from Muphrid. That charlatan Petro told you what you wanted to hear, and you all lapped it up. And what about the fifth precept: *Disdain those who concur. Honour those who dissent.* Were there no dissenting voices?"

Celeste. She had been a dissenting voice.

"Isolde..." Mila reached out to touch Isolde's arm and she jerked it angrily away.

"It's alright, Mila." Ilyas said. "Petro had a valid argument, Isolde. Everyone before us had spent their resources on running, not fighting. Petro's crime was to run away himself."

"Still you deceive yourself. For every one who could have left, hundreds would be left behind. Petro played on your secret fears. You would rather no one was saved than be left behind yourself. He was a devil of your own making." Isolde backed her chair from the table. "I'm tired, Mila. Help me to my bed."

Ilyas cleared the table — the mechs would have done it, but it kept him busy while Mila helped Isolde. He waited for her outside the door. A clear night revealed the tracery of street lights on the habitat's far side, with dark patches of parks, all cut through with the arrow-straight silhouette of the darkened sun-tube.

Disdain those who concur. Honour those who dissent. The dissenters at Muphrid were all silenced, or had silenced themselves, like Celeste.

105

"Isolde's asleep." Mila appeared at his elbow. "She was sharp tonight." Her hand reached for his.

"Tomorrow." He clasped his hands behind his back. "I'd like to go to my ship."

Mila cast her eyes down. "OK. I understand."

Before bed, Ilyas sat alone in his living room gazing through the aurocular. At the star map, and through the eyes of Thurlina's sensors that waited patiently for the coming of the Enemy.

His dreams that night took him back to Muphrid, where he wandered the empty streets past the flight school, through abandoned parks and into the echoing emptiness of the great hall, finally climbing the stairs to his apartment on the fourth floor of the ziggurat. He found Celeste reading her book, lying in the bath of crimson water.

"You're too late," she said.

"Too late for what?"

"You killed us all, now it's time."

"Why do you say that. Why say that *I* killed everyone?"

"Look in the mirror."

Ilyas felt the presence of the mirror behind him, the mirrored door of the small cabinet over the sink. He didn't want to turn, didn't want to look.

"Look in the mirror!"

Her words compelled him, unwilling, he turned. A familiar face stared back; thick grey hair, broad features, stern expression. Marshal Petro.

"Now," Celeste's voice reverberated from the bathroom tiles. "It's time."

Ilyas woke to the sound of a distant siren. He slipped on the aurocular to see Thurlina's sensors scintillating with gravity waves from every direction. The Enemy was here. Only hours remained before the hail of hypervelocity projectiles would shatter the habitat's silicate shell. He rose from his bed, washed and dressed, and made his way out into the dim light of night. In the adjacent dwelling, Isolde's frail form lay still as stone in her bed. Her implant had fulfilled its intended purpose and spared her pain, the stilling of her weak heart an unfortunate side effect.

He sat a moment with her, replaying her words of the previous evening. *Honour those who dissent.*

In the next house, Mila breathed softly in her sleep. He touched her hand. "Mila," he whispered, but she did not stir. In the darkness of her bedroom Ilyas searched for his anger but found only the image of Marshal Petro's face staring at him from the mirror in his dream.

A word to Ilyas's aurocular summoned a transit car which took him the short distance from the hospital to the end cap before rising up the slope into the open between fields and vineyards. Quickly, the climb steepened until it ascended the vertical face to the axis, weight declining to nothing, then out through the hub into windowless passages, a maze of pressurised tubes that spidered out from the axis to the zero-g docks, workshops, and freight and passenger terminals.

It stopped in an embarkation hall. Long glass windows on one side looked out on the aged and pitted outer wall of the habitat's end-cap, its motion barely visible as it turned beneath. The docks extended out past the window on the other side: lattices of struts with clamps and docking ports, all empty but the one where Ilyas's ship sat. Tiny, patched and battered, but whole.

The weight of his burden had slowed him on the walk from Mila's dwelling to the transit, and the inertia of it made him clumsy as he manoeuvred without gravity along the tube to the docking port. Ilyas squeezed through the open hatch and into the cramped cockpit. A systems check showed the reactor on-line, the ship ready, the range-limit still disabled. He prepared a navigation program so that when he began the launch sequence the hatch would close, the clamps release. A short spurt from the thrusters and the ship would clear the dock and make the jump to the Zosma system. Seven years would elapse; the blink of an eye in subjective time.

Little time remained, but enough for the burden that waited in the access tube. A few moments and he was finished. Ilyas reached across the cramped space of the cockpit to press the button to begin the launch sequence. As the hatch closed he made his way back to the embarkation hall to watch the departure through the long window.

This time, he would treat the world as it was. What did it matter where Petro had fled, if he had escaped at all? Ilyas had constructed an impeccable chain of logic that would lead him to Zosma, as impeccable as the logic of defending Muphrid had been. Petro had been Ilyas's own creation. His, and all those who had stood in the great hall with him.

This time, someone would be saved, someone would survive at least until the next roll of the dice. In seven years elapsed, hours subjective, the sedative would wear off and Mila Kraft would awaken in the cockpit of his ship looking out at the colonies at Zosma.

"Stand or fall." Ilyas folded his arms and waited.

See David Whitmarsh's story "Stand or Fall" online at Metaphorosis.
If you liked it, leave a comment. Authors love that!
Remember to subscribe to our e-mail updates so you'll know when new stories are posted.

About the story

This story began life as an exercise in filling the backstory of a character in an as yet unpublished novel that follows the fate of two thousand refugees who escape the Enemy's attack on Zosma, one of the last of humanity's settled systems. Mila Kraft, who is sent by Ilyas to Zosma at the end of this story, is one of the main characters; a doctor who is older than she looks, and follows the syntheist faith but is sympathetic to the Covenant. I started by thinking about how she acquired all those attributes.

The Enemy's assault on humanity lies in the past in the novel, forming part of the background. Writing this story gave me a chance to play with ideas about how different societies, isolated from each other by the light-speed limit on travel and communication, would react in different ways to the inexorable advance on an invincible enemy.

The first draft almost wrote itself in just a few days. The mechanics of the story came together easily, but it has taken many revisions and much valued feedback from others to develop and clarify Ilyas's arc.

A question for the author

Q: What's better: writing or having written?

A: Writing, by far. I get great pleasure from creating new worlds, working them out in more detail than ever reaches the page, then populating them with characters that I move through the arcs of their stories. Once having written, it's just time to move onto the next thing. Better than having written, is having been read.

About the author

David Whitmarsh is a rehabilitated software engineer who now spends his days playing acoustic blues badly and writing. David lives in West Sussex with his wife, two cats and a varying subset of his four adult children.

@whitmarshdj

Gatekeepers

Douglas DiCicco

Now she'd never get to finish her book, Elsie thought. She'd just gotten to the good bit when her train derailed.

"So what happens now?" she asked Osiris. "You weigh my heart against a feather?"

"Not personally, no," Osiris answered. "Too many dead people these days. The gatekeepers handle that now. I just get the process started."

Osiris reached into Elsie's chest and pulled out her heart. It was more colorful than Elsie would have guessed, much more luminous. Her heart was a whirl of metallic sheens and colorful glows.

"What did you love most in life?" Osiris asked, eyes on the heart.

"Stories," Elsie answered.

Osiris smiled and pressed the heart into Elsie's hands. It squelched with disconcerting wetness.

"I'd start there." Osiris pointed down one of the countless corridors stretching endlessly into the dark in every direction. Like all the others, it was lined with shadowy figures, each standing before a flickering portal. "Third on the left. Best of luck."

Elsie followed the directions. She felt her heartbeat quicken in her hands. She was nervous.

The third shade on the left hovered before a portal to an endless library. Up close, Elsie could smell tea and paper wafting through.

"Do you seek to take your eternal rest in my realm?" the shade asked.

"I think so?" Elsie answered. She wasn't quite certain how all this worked.

The answer seemed to be enough for the shade. It took Elsie's heart from her and held it up to the light. It turned the heart from side to side, then upside down. The shade shook its head disapprovingly. "No, no. I'm sorry. This won't do at all."

"Why not?" Elsie frowned.

"See this bit here?" The shade tapped at a silver bit on the heart's underside. It produced a quiet metallic ping. "Dragon scale. Or some other mythical creature. Doesn't matter." The shade passed the heart back, handling it like a scrap of rotten fish it was eager to be rid of. "If it's part of your heart, I can't let you pass."

"Why does that matter?" Elsie asked.

The shade sighed. "Because this is the portal to the Realm of Literary Readers," it answered. "Literary." The shade repeated the word, emphasizing each and every syllable. "This is a place for the souls of serious readers of serious works."

"I like serious literature," Elsie insisted.

"Yes, but you also like dragons. Or something just as bad. Something that smacks of genre." The shade said. "I'm sorry, but there's no place for you in my realm. Try the Realm of Fantasy Readers." It stretched out a shadowy limb. "Down that way, fifth on the right."

Elsie took the advice and presented her heart to the shade guarding the portal to the Realm of Fantasy Readers. It was just as unimpressed as the first shade had been. "No, I'm sorry. I don't think this is the place for you."

"The last one I spoke with thought it was," Elsie said. "They said there's a dragon scale on my heart."

"What, this?" The new shade poked at the heart's silver bit. "Oh, no. That's no dragon scale. No, looks like chrome to me. You probably want the Realm of Cyberpunk Readers. Back the way you came. Second on your left."

The guardian of the Realm of Cyberpunk Readers was no more receptive to Elsie's heart. "The hearts of true cyberpunk aficionados are wrought of naught but chrome and bleed naught but code. Look, you've got this much larger dark patch right here." It prodded a particularly squishy portion of the heart. "I'd try Horror Readers."

The shade at the portal to the Realm of Horror Readers weighed Elsie's heart and found it too light. The guardian of the Realm of Comedy Readers weighed it again, and found it too heavy. Her heart was too cold for Erotica, too hot for Cozy Mysteries. Elsie's heart was too old-fashioned for Science Fiction, too modern for Alternate History.

"Have you tried the Realm of Literary Readers?" suggested the shade guarding the Realm of Thriller Readers, after a rejection full of misdirection and shocking twists.

Elsie slumped against the wall, knees against her chest, clutching her heart tightly. She had wandered the endless halls for what felt like an eternity. She felt no closer to finding the place she belonged. Each of the realms had something which drew her in, but the shades barred her way at every turn.

"Still here?"

Elsie looked up to see Osiris offering her a hand. She took it and got back to her feet. "I don't belong anywhere." she said, barely holding back tears.

Osiris smiled gently. "Which stories were your favorites?"

Elsie considered the question for a moment. "The ones I told myself."

"Ah." Osiris gave Elsie's hand a gentle squeeze. "Come with me."

Osiris led her to a portal guarded by a squat and smoky shade.

"Try this one." Osiris suggested.

Elsie stepped forward. She could hear the scribbling of pens and the clacking of typewriters echoing from the portal. She smelled good coffee and cheap whisky. She glimpsed untidy desks overflowing with crumpled notes and obscure reference tomes. The portal beckoned to her like none of the others had.

"Do you seek to take your eternal rest here, in the Realm of Writers?" the shade asked, holding out a shadowy tendril.

"Yes." Elsie said, handing over her heart.

The shade inspected the heart. The parade of rejections had drained Elsie's heart of much of the energy and vigor it once possessed. It was a dark, shriveled thing now, hard and bitter, like an especially withered raisin.

"It certainly looks like a writer's heart," the shade said. It placed the heart on a shelf beside the portal. "Thank you for your interest in the Realm of Writers. You can expect an answer in six to eight weeks."

Elsie sat before the shade and waited. She waited, and waited, and waited. Six weeks passed. Then eight. Then twelve. It was somewhere around half a year when the shade finally picked her heart off the shelf, eyeballed it for a moment, then tossed it back to Elsie.

"Thank you for your submission to the Realm of Writers." The shade sounded very rehearsed. "Unfortunately, your heart does not meet our realm's needs at the present moment."

"What?" Elsie cried. She'd really thought this would be the one.

"We receive many quality hearts of the recently deceased," the shade continued. "I'm afraid your heart didn't quite win me over. I wish you the best of luck finding another placement for your eternal soul."

Elsie sat there a moment, stunned, staring at the withered lump her heart had become. She had no idea what to do now, where to go. This was the only place that had felt right for her, and now it was closed off. Not knowing what else to do, she got back to her feet and prepared to resume what felt like a futile search.

"Didn't like this one after all?" Osiris was back.

"I don't belong here either," Elsie said, holding back tears.

Osiris arched an eyebrow. "Says who?"

Elsie pointed to the shade in front of the portal.

"Ah." Osiris smiled. "You know... they're only as strong as you let them be."

Elsie watched the shade for a moment. When she turned back to Osiris, they had already disappeared.

She looked down at the heart in her hands. She saw a flicker of light somewhere deep in the core. A spark that hadn't quite been snuffed out. She turned back to the portal and marched forward.

"You again." The shade seemed both surprised and mildly annoyed. "I'm sorry, I can't provide personal feedback on each and every heart I examine. If you'd like to try again with a new core personal identity, maybe something a little more mainstream, I'd be happy to review another submission."

Elsie ignored the shade and kept moving toward the portal. Her heart glowed brighter.

"Wait!" The shade moved to block Elsie from the portal. "You can't go in. You aren't a real writer. I haven't approved you yet."

Elsie held up her heart. The light shone straight through the shade. She walked through it, ignoring the guardian's wailing as she entered the portal.

"This time..." Elsie said as the light enveloped her. "I'm going to write my own ending."

See Douglas DiCicco's story "Gatekeepers"
online at Metaphorosis.
If you liked it, leave a comment. Authors love
that!
Remember to subscribe to our e-mail updates so
you'll know when new stories are posted.

About the story

The world of fiction is full of gatekeepers, from editors of major publications to social media trolls who take it upon themselves to police who counts as a "real" fan of their genre. This can be demoralizing not only to writers, but to readers. This story came from taking that problem to an extreme, and thinking about the ways people can respond to it.

A question for the author

Q: Do you have any pets? Do they influence your writing?

A: I have no pets at the moment, but I've had many over the years: a dog, three cats, two parakeets. Like any part of the family, pets shape your whole view of the world. That can't help but influence your writing.

About the author

Douglas DiCicco is an author of speculative fiction living in Clovis, California. He has worked as an attorney, a teacher, and a Renaissance Faire performer.

@CiccoDouglas

Tides

Ailsa Bristow

The woman stood at the edge of a cliff, suspended halfway between sky and sea. At her back, beyond the rocky outcrop, was the ancient cottage, shutters clattering with the ocean breeze.

She breathed the world in. There had been a storm last night, and the world was salt-scrubbed clean. She watched the sun begin to roll over the horizon, painting the sky in hazy yellows and soft pinks. It was a day for starting over.

She began to walk. Her legs were still stiff, foreign things, and she stumbled a little at first, but soon found her stride. She tried not to think about the old man she'd left behind in the cottage. In the inside pocket of the windbreaker he'd loaned her was a thick roll of green bills that she'd found in a kitchen drawer that morning.

She walked. The skin on her hands blackened with dirt that she stooped to gather by the fistful for no other reason than to inhale its foreign fragrance. She walked, letting the roar of the sea grow more distant with every step. The land seemed quiet until she trained herself to listen for the furtive creatures burrowing in the earth and to hear the wind singing in the trees. From time to time, she spotted the dim shapes of squat buildings in the distance. She avoided them, her stomach clenching as she remembered the way the old man's eyes had crinkled as he smiled.

Perhaps it was better not to risk getting too close to other strangers.

She walked.

As she walked, she gathered new words, fragments of overheard stories, questions. Her days were loose. She might rest beneath the shade of a beech tree for hours or run as fast as she could just to feel the way the wind tugged at her hair. She slept in barns and in hollows and, once, in the bed of a pick-up truck, where the blankets she found felt like a gift, just for her. She slipped among the people whose words she ate up, who shared food with her, always a passer-by. She thought she might keep herself safe, that way.

When she arrived in the city it was airless, choked with dust and fumes. She almost turned around and walked straight back the way she had come, ready to give up on whatever impulse had brought her this far. Only curiosity forced her feet forward.

She wanted more stories. She wanted answers.

There were words for what she'd done. She was a runaway, a fugitive, a thief. But none of the words seemed to fit right; they cut tight against her skin.

She had been seeking solid ground for a long time. Not even the ocean had been wide or deep enough to contain her restless heart.

Her mother, her voice crashing and roaring, had told her: "This is who you are. This is where you belong."

Though it had never been spoken between them, she knew her mother was lying. Or at least, she wasn't telling the whole truth. There was another world she belonged to. It didn't matter that the ocean was her home, her inheritance. It was also her prison.

Without meaning to, she had found the beach—colliding fragments of all that made her: salt, shadow, stillness. She was transmogrified; fresh bone grazing against socket; new skin tested by sharp rocks. Her untested lungs had choked on cooling air.

Her mother roared in fury as her wayward daughter scrambled along the beach. Wave after wave lashed her legs, tried to pull her back in. She had dug her fingers into the grit and damp of the sand. Her hands had found rocks, a way to tether herself to the land. When the old man found her, she was still clinging to them, the skin on her palms red and raw.

The old man had lived his whole life by the sea. She could smell it on him. He ought to have known enough stories to warn him away from beautiful young women washed up on the shore. Still, he had covered her with his jacket, and offered her his hand, and she had taken it, pulling herself up and away from the sand, the stone, the water.

She tried not to think of how much of herself she might have left behind.

The cottage was ancient—too few windows, and all of them small—but comfortable enough. In the kitchen, plates and bowls were stacked on every surface; spoiling fruit spilled out of a bowl, but the fridge was bare and empty.

"Sorry," the old man said, with a vague wave of the hand. "Since my wife died, I've not had much company."

He'd fumbled through the cupboards, at last pulling out a battered box of pasta and a dusty jar of sauce.

"I'm sorry," she said. "About your wife."

His jaw tightened. "S'alright," he mumbled, but she could read the grief in his face: the way his eyes seemed to look just past her when he spoke, the rumpled shirt, the hollows of his cheeks.

"Tell me a story," she said, and, as they sat down to eat the pasta he had cooked until flaccid, he had.

There was a young man, lived round these parts. Fisherman by trade. Cut him open

and his veins would have run with salt water, that's right. He knew the water like a husband knows his wife. Knew just by looking at the water when a squall was coming. Knew never to set sail on a Friday, knew never to tempt the winds by whistling when at sea. Knew the sea for a goddess, and a fearsome one at that, and knew enough not to scoff at the devotions the older men made as they set sail, even though they were good Christians when they set foot back on the land.

And the young man fell in love with sea. Even when he was not out to fish, he would journey out in his boat, to admire the glimmer of sunlight upon the waves. When the water was calm, he'd let the little boat drift, and let his fingers run back and forth through the icy waters, a caress. When a storm blew, he roared along with the sea, his heart thrumming.

And the sea, in her own way, loved him too. Loved the solidity of him, loved his quick-quick energy. Loved his youth and his wonder, loved the startling blue of his eyes.

One day, a storm caught the young fisherman off-guard—the swelling waves tugged him in towards a sandbar, tossed the boat over jagged rocks.

The fisherman ought to have died, but the sea, well she scooped him up. Carried him to a cove and forced herself—at great cost—to join him on the shore, so she could pump the water from his lungs. Kept his frozen body warm with her own body, pressed a kiss to his raw and bloody lips.

She had waited, unwilling to speak lest she break the story's spell, but the man's voice had faded and drifted. The light outside the cottage died and the *plink plink plink* of rain against glass filled the silence between them.

"And?" she asked when she could bear it no longer. "What happened next?"

The old man startled, blinked at her as if he'd forgotten she was there. His hand grazed the rough stubble on his chin.

"The story ends the way all stories about love must end," the man said, his smile wry. "Tragedy and loss." He'd shifted abruptly out of his chair, began to gather the plates from dinner. She hurried to help him; her hands clumsy as she dried the heavy pan. When the task was done, the old man stood staring at his hands, pruned by the dish water. He didn't look up, but when he spoke it was clearly: "Still, better to have loved and lost. Better to have loved and lost."

The city invited strangers. She noticed the way the people moved through it and left only the barest of traces. A damp palm print on a revolving door, the lingering smell of perfume in a bathroom stall.

The city was a place to disappear into; a place where she could have a life of her own making.

She became skilled at getting by. She learned how to take favours without giving up too much of herself. Learned the city's rhythm, grew used to the heat of so many bodies pressed up against one another. Learned how, sometimes, if she looked into someone's eyes for just the right amount of time, they would forget what she'd neglected to pay for. They always sent her off with a smile.

Still, it didn't matter how far she had travelled from the ocean. She woke sometimes to the sound of crashing waves. The water in her bathroom sink ran thick with salt, coating the basin with crystals. When she walked down the grey city streets seagulls as lost as she was cried out, *come home, home come home, come, come.*

A man with eyes the colour of moss approached her in a bar.

"Adam," he said, sticking out his hand. She couldn't help but smile at his boyish bravado. She gave him a name, let him buy her a drink.

He asked her where home was.

"That's a complicated question," she said, and he nodded as if he understood. He told her about the place where he grew up. The landlocked mountains where rock hemmed in the sky. He told her about driving up mist-skirted highways, passing trees standing sentinel.

"A place like that gets in your bones," he said. "I'll never leave it."

He had a habit of running his hand through his brown hair, leaving it sticking out in every direction. He shook his head and gave a wry laugh. "I think I've had one too many," he said, tipping his empty glass.

"No," she said. "No, I know exactly what you mean." Her eyes slid away. "I'd love to see the mountains, someday."

They left together, drunk and laughing. She let him into her damp basement apartment. Her eyes followed his as he took in the bare walls, the single bed, the wilting flowers on the kitchen counter.

"How long did you say you'd been here?"

She didn't answer, and when she kissed him, he tasted of pine.

Adam fit into her life in ways she hadn't known she needed. Together, they painted her apartment. She spent hours agonizing over paint chips until she at last selected a white called *fresh start*. Adam laughed. He arrived at her door week after week with his arm full of plants—cacti, palms, rubber plants, succulents, spider plants— until her apartment brimmed with green.

"Things even you can't kill," he said with a grin.

He cooked her breakfast and as she ate, he read her the headlines, his face reddening as he unspooled all the trouble in the world.

She asked him for a story, and he laughed, asked "What *kind* of story?" and looked baffled when she shrugged and said, "Any kind of story." He sat in silent thought for a minute. When he began to speak, his dark brows pinched together in concentration.

When I was a kid, my dad couldn't work out how he ended up with a wimp like me. I'd cry at anything: a dead racoon at the side of the road, the thought of puppies being separated from their mothers, a harsh word from a kid at school. My mom called me sensitive *but, my dad… well. He wanted to protect me, I guess. Signed me up for judo, got me into weightlifting, gave me my first sip of beer when I was 12 years old. He loved me in his own way, I think.*

So anyway, when I was sixteen, dad and I went on a camping trip. It was the thing we'd always shared. We loved the crisp mountain air, loved bathing in still, crystal clear lakes. We'd spend our days hiking, gathering firewood, making camp, maybe fishing. At night, my dad would whittle and tell me all about his dad, his childhood, the kind of things we never normally talked about.

On the last night, he told me he was sick. There wasn't much that could be done, he said. A few months, maybe half a year. And I cried. Of course I did, as if I were splitting into a million pieces. He hugged me tight, and I could smell the salt-sweat of his skin, the lingering sunscreen, the sweet mildewy scent of his clothes. His hands were rough, and red, and he gripped me so hard it was as though he thought he could hold me together through sheer force of will. He held me until I had nothing more in me, until I was empty and stunned.

It was a clear night, the stars sprawled out across the velvet sky. My dad still held me close.

Finally, he said, "You can't care this much, son. You can't keep living life with your heart on your sleeve. The world'll destroy you if you care too much."

I didn't know what to say to that and so I said nothing. Six weeks later, he was dead.

Adam worked as a government relations officer at a large non-profit. As they spent more time together, her space began to fill with briefing papers and glossy reports, printouts of statistical models, survey data sets. He dressed every morning in his grey dress pants and when she saw him in the evenings his tie was always loose, his shirt sleeves rolled up. He'd seemed baffled when she told him that she worked odd jobs—catering shifts and office temp work, mostly—couldn't understand her lack of drive, ambition.

"Maybe I've had enough of ambition for one lifetime," she'd said. "Maybe I want to paint on a smaller canvas."

The truth was, she liked to be anonymous, forgettable. She sailed through galas and parties, tray of canapes balanced in one hand, offering guests an impassive smile. All the while, her mind floated away.

In her new life, she was slow, dreamy. She lost hours gathering stories, imagining new possibilities. She wrote herself into many different futures: a house with Adam, two kids and a dog; a lonely mountaintop cabin where she would paint and write; a bustling farmhouse, full of friends and guests, honeysuckle creeping up the walls.

"You have enough energy for the both of us," she'd tell Adam with a playful nudge. "You change the world. I'm just trying to live in it."

Still, it rankled. To spend time with Adam was to be recruited into his causes. Housing accessibility and playground regeneration. Traffic calming and environmental justice. Once, she even found him furiously typing on a neighbourhood Facebook page, dedicated to saving the local Starbucks.

Her burbling laugh had been cut short by the look on his face. It was the most accessible coffee shop in the area, he'd told her, lonely young moms used it, it was a safe place for homeless people. "Community spaces *matter*," he'd said, his cheeks stained red.

One morning she woke to find his face bathed in the blue light from his phone. His hair was matted to one side of his head, and she could trace the lines of the pillow creases across his cheeks. He propped himself up on an elbow, thrust the phone at her. "Look at this," he demanded. She stared at the image of a beached whale, its body swollen and grotesque against the white sand.

She looked away. "Do you have to—"

"This is *happening*," he said. "Right here, right now. It's our duty to look. To do something."

She rolled out of bed, backed away from him and the photo he was still brandishing at her. "What are you doing? This isn't *doing* anything," she spat.

She'd left as he'd continued to lecture her, picking up her bag and slamming the door shut behind her. She didn't return until the sun began to bruise in the sky.

Adam was sat there on the steps that led up to her apartment, eyes rimmed with red, stubble skimming his chin.

She waited as he pushed himself up, ran a hand through his wild hair. Everything they'd said and everything they'd left unsaid hung between them.

And then he closed the space between them, pulled her into a tight embrace. "Don't you ever do that again; do you hear me?" His voice was thick with his too-ready tears. "I thought—"

But she didn't let him finish, pressed her mouth against his lips. As they made their way back into the apartment, she thought about the yoke of belonging to someone; of the obligation that came from holding another person's happiness between your hands.

Despite everything, they *were* happy. Her happiness was physical, solid, lodged beneath her ribcage. Happiness was a kind of pain. Adam's eyes, his smile, his hand grazing hers—her happiness tended to be a sharp-clawed thing that seemed to press against her ribs. She was afraid—if she let her happiness loose, would it crack her open? Would it gut her?

In the cool blue light of a morning, she thought about ending things. She could form the words so easily, knew how his face would crumple, knew how he would fight back the tears. Would he be gentle in the face of heartbreak? Would he shout and slam the door on their life together? When he told the story to their friends would he cast her as the villain?

Sleepy, he rolled over in the bed, pulled her into his body. His eyes blinked open.

"What's this?" he asked, brushing a thumb over her damp cheeks.

"I just..." The words lodged in her throat. How could she tell him all the ways she'd fought to get free, only to find herself clutching him?

"I don't want to leave you," she choked out.

Adam searched her face, his gaze gentle. He planted a kiss on her forehead, rested his chin there. "So don't," he said, as if it were that simple. Her body shook with the force of a sadness that needed to crash over rocks.

"You don't understand," she whispered. "Where I come from... I'll never leave there. I'll always being going back there. And that means..."

He cupped her chin in his palms. "Means you'll have to leave me?"

She nodded; her throat too closed for words.

He considered her. "You talk as if there's no choices to be made, love."

Her mother's voice echoed on her tongue. "I'm flighty, selfish. I'll never settle down, never take things seriously."

Adam pulled back. His thumb gently nudged her chin until she met his gaze. "That's not you. That's not who you are." He was close enough for his breath to warm her skin. "You can promise me right now. Whatever choices we make, we'll make them together."

Pine and salt, leaves rustling and the crash of waves. Her thoughts tangled, but he didn't release her from his arms and so she nodded. "I promise."

Days passed, weeks passed, months passed, and she stayed.

She and Adam moved into to a house with a garden that she did not know how to tend. They visited farmer's markets, they argued over who had or had not taken out the garbage, they filled their house with the laughter and shouting of friends who believed that a good argument over wine would be enough to put the world to rights.

And Adam grew used to the way the gulls would line up along their back fence every morning.

They were building a life, she thought, day by day. She had never realized it would be so ordinary, so tedious, so beautiful.

They stretched out on their deck on a late July night, the plum sky shimmering with the light of the city. Heat pounded like a pulse through them. Adam rolled a joint as she sipped a glass of cool earthy wine.

They sank back into the pillows and blankets they'd pulled outside. They talked about taking a trip to the mountains—she'd still never seen the place where he was born.

Silence fell between them.

"You'll make a wonderful mother, one day."

His palm pressed against her thigh. She flinched but did not pull away.

"You don't want to?"

"No—I mean—I haven't really thought about it yet."

He rolled her onto her side so he could cradle her in his arms. "So... Think about it."

The story was almost too easy to write. Stacks of laundry. Toys underfoot. Counting steps and hopping over the cracks in the sidewalk. Naming all the animals in the city park zoo. Green eyes that would promise endless summer. A laugh that could crack a day wide open.

She could see it all.

She kissed him before she could say all that was in her heart.

The night breeze whispered *come home*. Water dripping from taps calling *come, come, come*. The gulls, once silent, began to caw, ever more insistent, *come home, home, home*. She tried to ignore it, but the message echoed across water as wide as continents, and over the windswept land.

Thin-lipped newscasters delivered the solemn news that the ocean was dying. Fish washed up rotting on the shoreline. The water stank of sulphur. Children foolish enough to splash in wading pools, lakes, or even puddles, appeared in emergency rooms, their skin blistering and black. There was no explanation; something had gone wrong. Adam read her the stories over their breakfast coffees until she at last begged him to stop.

"We have a duty," he said, frowning.

An argument years in the making echoed between them.

Rain drummed against the windows, *come home*. The wind howled, *come home*. She tossed in the bed, trying to sleep through the clamour of a storm until she heard in a roll of thunder the message she had been trying to ignore. *Your mother is dead. Come home.*

She forgot to eat. Her eyes, once deep blue, turned dishwater grey. Sentences, thoughts drifted away from her.

"What is it?" Adam asked her. He tried being gentle, but when he couldn't reach her the words became an accusation. "What's going on with you?"

It wasn't that she didn't want to tell him. It was that anytime she tried to fishhook the words up through her mouth, she found only breath and silence.

Come home, come home.

She dreamed of the old man, pictured the way he stood staring at his hands in the basin of soapy dishwater. *Better to have loved and lost*, he'd said. But he'd also told her all love stories ended in tragedy and loss.

She considered the weight of a lifetime of waiting.

Remembered the fractured sadness in the old man's deep blue eyes.

She woke to the sheets soaked and reeking of brine. Ice cold water flooded the lungs that were made for land and not sea. There was no seawall to hold the waters back; her body screamed at the shock and then turned numb.

She lurched from the bed, her breath rasping. Adam stumbled after her.

"What's happening?" His green eyes were wide as she began slinging her belongings into a backpack. "What's going on?"

She blinked up at him through salt-water tears. She forced the words out through numb lips. "I can't. I can't anymore."

His face shuttered.

He stood at the door as she struggled down the steps with the bag of things she knew she would not need for long.

He stood on the front step, rain soaking through his t-shirt, plastering his dark hair to his skull. She wanted to be strong enough to walk away without a backward glance, but she couldn't help herself. One last look.

His mouth twisted. "I suppose I should thank you," he said, his voice trembling. "You tried to warn me once, didn't you?" His fists clenched and she knew she had to listen to what came next.

She didn't have to wait for long. He heaved a breath, and she noticed his eyes full of tears he was fighting not to shed. Then, turning slightly to one side, no longer looking at her, he said, "Go then. I should've known all along that you're too selfish to love me back."

An old man approached from the distance.

"So, you're back," he said.

Tears slid down her face.

The old man knelt beside her and drew her close. She inhaled his warmth, the tang of his body. She pressed into his solid, human form. Her borrowed body shook—there was so much she must leave behind.

"Tell me a story," she said, her words thick with tears.

And so, he did. The story of the restless goddess of the sea who'd fallen in love with a mortal man. The child she'd borne him. The life they'd tried to make together, wedged between water, rock, and sky.

"It never could last. When she realized what would happen to the seas if she left them forever..." His voice cracked; his eyes turned misty. "She had a duty. She had to return to her home."

She swallowed the words down, let them seep into her marrow.

"Life had to go on, you understand. The man, he married, and the sea..." He kept his eye on the crashing waves. "The sea is the sea. She moves according to a pattern of tides."

She was silent for a while, listening to the barely perceptible flutter in her belly. "I thought I could belong here," she said. "But I think I always knew I'd return to the sea one day." Her voice was the crash of waves against rock.

"She loved you, you know," he said. "Would be proud to see the woman you've become."

The old man held her for one last breath, and then gently let her go.

She let herself go, unpicking sinew from bone, atom from atom. *I have a duty*, she whispered, as she stretched herself thin, until she became a net spread across the ocean. She pictured Adam's face, serious and pale, his eyebrows bunched over those green eyes. But the water needed her more. And so she let the currents pull her under, sinking and bobbing, until there was no difference between her and the waves that carried her.

*See Ailsa Bristow's story "Tides" online at
Metaphorosis.
If you liked it, leave a comment. Authors love
that!
Remember to subscribe to our e-mail updates so
you'll know when new stories are posted.*

About the story

I wrote the first draft of "Tides" in 2017. In its first
iterations, it was very closely focused on the unnamed
protagonist. I'm interested in questions of fate and
free will, what we inherit vs. what we choose for
ourselves. I wanted to explore a tense relationship
between mother and daughter, and explore the urge
to rebel against familial duty. And, because my brain is
my brain, the idea of a fairytale or myth made the
most sense to me.

I've always been fascinated by the sea: I remember
being told once that growing up in the UK you're never
more than 60 miles from the ocean. I love its beauty
and respect its power; and I love the stories and
legends that shape the way we look at the sea. I don't
think using the idea of the sea as a personified being
was a conscious choice, but something that just
clicked for me.

As the story grew and changed under multiple
revisions I know that many other themes that interest

me worked their way into the story. Both the protagonist and Adam have left their homes, and I look at the way they try to make a new home together in a place that neither of them belong to. I can see a lot of my own climate anxiety and feelings of powerlessness come through in Adam—the question that echoes beneath this story is, perhaps, what are we willing to sacrifice in order to do the right thing? Adam says all the right words, but it is the protagonist who ultimately gives up the things she has fought for so fiercely.

As a writer, I love working on the stories that feel like a mystery to me as they are being written. The process of revising this story has been a process of getting clearer and clearer about who these characters are, and why they make the choices they make. That these characters continue to live and breathe in my imagination, four years after they first took root there, seems to me part of the magic of being a writer.

A question for the author

Q: What is the first/most recent book that you lost sleep reading/thinking about?

A: I read Erin Morgenstern's *The Starless Sea* earlier this year and it's stayed with me. I loved how Morgenstern created this rich, vivid fantasy world that also tells us so much about our own world and what it means to be human. And I definitely did some writerly swooning over some of the sentences in that book! I highly recommend it, if you haven't already read it.

About the author

Ailsa Bristow is a British writer who grew up living at least half her time in the stories she created. Now she lives in Toronto, with her partner and their idiosyncratic but much loved cat, Steve. She continues to spend most of her time dreaming of other worlds.

www.ailsabristow.ca, @AilsaBristow

Copyright

Title information

Metaphorosis December 2021

ISSN: 2573-136X (online)
ISBN: 978-1-64076-213-8 (e-book)
ISBN: 978-1-64076-214-5 (paperback)

Copyright

Publisher

Metaphorosis Magazine is an imprint of
Metaphorosis Publishing
Neskowin, OR, USA

Discounts available

Substantial discounts are available for educational institutions, including writing workshops. Discounts are also available for quantity purchases. For details, contact Metaphorosis at metaphorosis.com/about

Metaphorosis Publishing

Metaphorosis offers beautifully written science fiction and fantasy. Our imprints include:

Metaphorosis Magazine
Plant Based Press
Verdage

You can also find us:
@MetaphorosisMag, @MetaphorosisRev,
@Metaphorosis
www.facebook.com/metaphorosis

Help keep Metaphorosis running by supporting us at
Patreon.com/metaphorosis

See more about some of our books on the following pages.

Metaphorosis
a magazine of speculative fiction

Metaphorosis is an online speculative fiction magazine dedicated to quality writing. We publish an original story every week, along with author bios, interviews, and notes on story origins.

We also publish monthly print and e-book issues, as well as yearly Best of and Complete anthologies.

Come and see us online at magazine.Metaphorosis.com

Metaphorosis: Best of 2020

The best science fiction and fantasy stories from *Metaphorosis* magazine's fifth year.

Metaphorosis 2020

All the stories from *Metaphorosis* magazine's fifth year. Fifty-two great SFF stories.

Metaphorosis: Best of 2019

The best science fiction and fantasy stories from *Metaphorosis* magazine's fourth year.

Metaphorosis 2019

All the stories from *Metaphorosis* magazine's fourth year. Fifty-two great SFF stories.

Metaphorosis: Best of 2018

The best science fiction and fantasy stories from *Metaphorosis* magazine's third year.

Metaphorosis 2018

All the stories from *Metaphorosis* magazine's third year. Fifty-two great SFF stories.

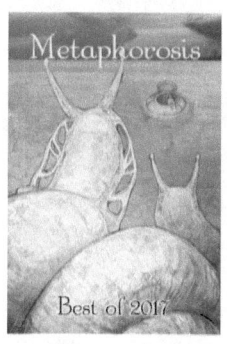

Metaphorosis:
Best of 2017

The best science
fiction and fantasy
stories from
Metaphorosis
magazine's *second*
year.

Metaphorosis
2017

All the stories
from *Metaphorosis*
magazine's second
year. Fifty-three
great SFF stories.

Metaphorosis: Best of 2016

The best science fiction and fantasy stories from *Metaphorosis* magazine's first year.

Metaphorosis 2016

Almost all the stories from *Metaphorosis* magazine's first year.

Plant Based Press

plant
based
press

Vegan-friendly science fiction and fantasy, including an annual anthology of the year's best SFF stories.

Best Vegan SFF of 2020

The best vegan-friendly science fiction and fantasy stories of 2020!

Best Vegan SFF of 2019

The best vegan-friendly science fiction and fantasy stories of 2019!

Best Vegan SFF of 2018

The best vegan-friendly science fiction and fantasy stories of 2018!

Best Vegan SFF of 2017

The best vegan-friendly science fiction and fantasy stories of 2017!

Best Vegan SFF of 2016

The best vegan-friendly science fiction and fantasy stories of 2016!

 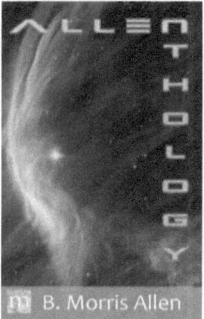

Susurrus

A darkly romantic story of magic, love, and suffering.

Allenthology: Volume I

A quarter century of SFF, including the full contents of the collections *Tocsin, Start with Stones,* and *Metaphorosis.*

Verdage

Science fiction and fantasy books for writers – full of great stories, often with an additional focus on the craft of speculative fiction writing.

Reading 5X5 x2

Duets

How do authors' voices change when they collaborate?

A round-robin of five talented science fiction and fantasy authors collaborating with each other and writing solo.

Including stories by Evan Marcroft, David Gallay, J. Tynan Burke, L'Erin Ogle, and Douglas Anstruther.

Score

an SFF symphony

What if stories were written like music? *Score* is an anthology of varied stories arranged to follow an emotional score from the heights of joy to the depths of despair – but always with a little hope shining through.

Reading 5X5

Five stories, five times

Twenty-five SFF authors, five base stories, five versions of each – see how different writers take on the same material.

Reading 5X5

Writers' Edition

Two extra stories, the story seed, and authors' notes on writing. Over 100 pages of additional material specifically aimed at writers.

Vestige

Novelettes, novellas, and novels by
Metaphorosis authors.